Oh the Audac

By Michael Colwill

First Published 2017

Copyright © Michael Colwill, 2017

Cartoon illustrations reproduced by permission
© Emma Parkinson, 2017 (all rights reserved)

Additional Original Drawings by Len

Forward

The title *Oh the Audacity* is a play on words and refers to the Aude department in South Western France; in times past this area was known as the Lauragaise.

The valley between Toulouse and the Narbonne formed part of it, and since the revolution, includes; the Haute Garonne, Arriege and Tarn.

With good soil, hot summers and large fields growing cereals, sunflowers and maize, this region is hugely agricultural; vines being grown on the poorer ground of the slopes producing the dark red wines of Corbieres and Minervois.

Historically this region was ravaged by the religious wars between the established Church of Rome and those holding the Cathar beliefs and frequently invaded and raided by marauders; many ruined castles outlined on rocky outcrops bearing witness to those troubled times.

This book however is about an invasion of a completely different kind; the invasion of this corner of France by a Cornishman, his family, and some of his friends who took and occupied one of the ruins...

Contents

1 - The Fateful Decision

The winter of January 1984 had taken a severe turn for the worse with the whole of Europe suffering exceptional and unusually cold weather. Icicles had been recorded on the palm trees at Nice and there had been many reported deaths amongst the old and infirm, people who had never experienced such low temperatures in their lives.

The housing market in England was once again in depression, and I had two renovated cottages and a new build house currently available for sale. The banks, in their usual manner, by charging excessive interest, were sucking equity out of the builders and landlords, including me, to enable them to load their bonuses!

The back problem that had dogged me for many years had reached a critical stage and I had been advised that some change would have to be taken in order to maintain any sort of active life.

Regular holiday breaks to the warmth in the south of Europe had proved to be a great relief, and my wife one Sunday, casting her eyes on a column in a Sunday newspaper on this significant afternoon spotted an advert:-

"Semi detached house for renovation in Aude SW France with planning permission to convert to a three bed roomed house. £5000"

She showed it to me, laughed and said, "that it didn't seem like a lot of money" but already my imagination was in overdrive, and from that moment the clock began ticking towards the greatest adventure of our lives.

There was a name and a French telephone number, and after much discussion, a decision was taken that "not much harm could come from making a phone call" and so it was duly made.

The resulting conversation only enhanced our interest, and I suggested to the vendors that I could find the time to fly out and view the property, to which they agreed.

Alex and I talked for maybe an hour, and our enthusiasm was growing by the minute. I could fly from Bristol to Toulouse where they would pick me up. I could sleep on a mattress at theirs for two or three nights and then return home. Make sure to dress for the conditions they said, as it was bitterly cold there, -20°c at night and the roads could be rather difficult, but they were confident of the journey, being now quite used to driving on ice after two weeks of practice. And so the die was cast.

The cold that hit me on my arrival at Toulouse took my breath away, but here I was in the south west of France in the coldest winter in memory, bowling along on a road of solid ice to view... What??

The journey to the village was marked by incredible pictures of trees in frozen relief, shining, and coated in glistening hoar frost and more beautiful than any decorated Christmas trees I had ever seen.

The route itself was a shining ribbon stretching ahead, and the drive lasted about an hour. When we reached the outskirts of Castelnaudary they said that this was where the difficult bit began. We now started the slow climb up the lower slopes of the Pyrenees towards our destination, 17 km to the village.

We arrived late in the evening and during a supper of pate and bread, and talking to my hosts Cher and Don, I realised that their project here was foundering for lack of funds, and the house that they were in the midst of renovating was needing more capital from the sale of their other property in order to complete it.

Their situation seemed to be dire, and worryingly for me, their reliance on my presence seemed to be far too important. Ah well, we'll see what tomorrow brings. That night was too cold to undress, so boots off, and quickly under the covers on a mattress on the floor for what was to be a restless night.

I lay there slowly recovering and warming through, and listening to the melancholy clang, clang, of the church bell, marking the passing of the night, eventually dropping off to sleep. In the morning, movement and the smell of coffee stirred me, and seeing daylight at 7.00 on a French morning was a bit of a surprise.

Rising and looking out of the window I got my first sighting of The village. Yes, run down and as yet no sign of life, the church looked very large, grey and forbidding as many French small village churches do. There was a primary school across the square but obviously there were no children apparent at this hour.

At the end of this row of houses stood a huge dilapidated, half timbered Elizabethan style building three stories high. The cemetery gate was to the side and one could see over the wall the tops of tombs and graves of the families of this area.

The privations suffered by my hosts would no doubt be bearable in fair weather but in this winter they were tough. They had installed a log burner in the living room of this rented house, which they had planned to remove to the cottage they were renovating at a later date, At the moment though it was their singular source of heat in this home, and a mobile gas grill being the only cooking appliance.

Barbeques at this moment seemed to be a very distant luxury and I was blessing the fact that I would not be the one waiting for them!

Well, we had bread, confitures and coffee to start our day and then, because they knew I was anxious to see what it was they had on offer for £5000. We coated and booted and stepped out into the winter wonderland.

We headed across the square towards the huge building that I have previously mentioned. My heart had already started sinking; it could not be could it? Well no actually it wasn't, but attached to it, at the near end was a semi-attached ruin without a roof, and yes this was it. Hellfire big problem! No way! I now had to work out how to let them down gently, although one suspects they may have already read my body language.

We moved on past what we now know as the old forge, to look at their other project further over, which was backing on to the cemetery. This was the cottage they had started renovating to be their home. It was a complete rebuild in progress, having no roof, three partial walls and a pile of stones of an original cottage. There seemed to be evidence of fire damage here at some time, which had caused discolouration to a quantity of these stones.

The floors were already screeded out and the front wall was mostly complete, the main supports for the second storey were partially in place as a platform, and some wiring under the screed was evident. Mains water and electricity were both already available on the site. All the timber was there and included double glazed windows, doors and all sinks, toilets, shower and bidets all of which were covered and listed. All the electric boxes and cable, and plumbing pipes, joints and taps were also there.

They showed me their plans with elevations when completed. It was well thought out and cleverly conceived. We spent a moment discussing it, and of course the joke about the quiet neighbours came up!

I told them that I needed time to think through their proposition, which actually meant I was flunking out by deferring my decision nearer to the point of my return. Coward that I am: It would give me a night to reflect on the madness of the idea and to find a way to let them down as gently as possible. So an uncomfortable night was in prospect, but slowly an idea was forming in my head.

The semi they were selling, attached to the Old Forge was certainly not going to be for me, definitely not on. It would be absolute madness, as the old structure was very nearly past the point of no return. The far end looked dangerous to me and could topple into the square at any time. The ground floor of this part of the building, they told me, had been a blacksmiths work shop, which later evolved to become an agriculture engineering business, reflecting the progression of agriculture back in the days when the village was self sufficient.

The owner had long been retired, but still lived in the village and was very well thought of by all.

But what of the project they had already started? It was detached. Planning permission had already been approved; most of the materials for the project were on site. A "kit house" with everything there necessary to continue and complete the build! I was quite sure they would not go for the option of selling it to me, but they were desperate and I would offer a fair price to take into account their initial work and concept.

I mulled and dozed for the rest of that troubled night and after a nervous and polite breakfast; I said I was ready to talk. I started immediately with the bad news and although somewhat crestfallen, they took it very well and I then continued with the "but". I outlined the possibility of buying their project in its present form, with all the materials as a complete lot.

I sensed a lightening of mood and after a long look at each other; they said "what would you offer?" I suggested a fair figure for the cottage and the "kit" to be added at cost. There was a very quiet pause and then Don said they would have to discuss it at length and we would talk again at lunch.

I spent the morning walking around the village, and admiring the display that this unusual spell of the winter had produced: Icicles, trees in shining relief in the sun, but still too cold to break its hold. It was an area well populated with hawks and I noticed much evidence of the devastation on the small bird population, who had no chance in this weather.

Nature can be a hard master but returning back across the square to the dilapidated door of the semi I had been offered, I spotted a pink rose bud encased and framed in ice, which was significantly offering both sadness and also promise for the future.

2 - A Major Celebration

(Which passed rather quickly!)

I have no memory of what we had for lunch that day as before we had started eating Don said "we agree to your offer and will be adding up all the accounts of the materials on site in order to give you the total." I was rather stunned and suffering from shock but just shook hands and suggested a visit to a restaurant in Castelnaudary that evening to celebrate and clinch the deal.

Cher said she would organise the evening and that we would gather together and be ready to leave about six o'clock. Totally dazed I left the table to re-examine once more what I had committed myself to, and to dream of a future of hot, dusty summers in this forgotten village in the foothills of the Pyrenees. Walking slowly across the square I was asking myself, was I fit for it? Doubtful, but when had I ever stepped back from anything? Was it a sound financial investment? Not to make a quick profit but probably recoverable. Did I want the challenge? Without a doubt! Just the sort of mad scheme that a West Country farmer turned restaurateur, turned developer now needed in his mid-life crisis!

The rest of my stay there in the village was spent in this haze, but later, in the afternoon we did make a visit to a notaire in Belpech where I left a British cheque written out in French Francs, which I would need to explain to my bank in England upon my return!

Later in Castelnaudary (somewhat sleepy in the depths of winter) there were a lot of uniformed troops about, and it was explained to me that the French Foreign Legion had their recruitment and training headquarters here. The Canal Du Midi meandered through the lower part of the town and I could imagine a huge change in activities here in the summer with a mooring "basin" busy and full of visitors in pleasure boats and barges.

We returned to the town that evening to a Hotel Restaurant where a table had been reserved for us. The meal and the evening were very pleasant, but of all the things to choose from the menu, I picked moules as a starter. You may realise that we were some distance from the coast and the best moules come from the West coast of Northern France.

The return to the village was uneventful and we retired to sleep. I didn't feel too comfortable but thought perhaps I had overeaten. At this stage I should perhaps explain that the privations of my host's house included an Elsan toilet (seated bucket) by the far wall of the bedroom. The feeling of discomfort now took a serious turn for the worse and developed into severe stomach cramps and a growing impression of nausea. I hurried to the toilet in time to vomit and lost, what I imagined to be, the whole meal we had consumed that evening. Still feeling really groggy I returned to lie down, but the stomach cramps had returned and after an uncomfortable hour I realised that I must go to the dreaded toilet once more, but on this occasion to sit down and my need was getting more urgent by the second. I scrambled up, lurched across to the WC and in panic began pulling down and off with my heavy clothing. The problem was, at the point of sitting I had another cramp and before my backside had found a base, lost control and my bowels vented themselves with great force behind me! The noise all this made will haunt me for the rest of my life and I stayed sitting on the toilet with my head in my hands hardly caring at my predicament, or the mess that I would view on rising and turning. I was certainly rueing my choice of moules now, but the worse did seem to be over as I had cleared out most of the problem! I struggled to my feet and after cleaning myself up pulled my clothes back on as I was by now feeling very cold, which was of no great help: With some trepidation I turned to view the damage I had caused.

Unbelievably, the temperature was so cold that "it" had frozen solid on hitting the wall and lay there in one big slab! Relieved in more than one way, I resumed a broken and quite miserable night knowing that this news had to be imparted to my hosts in the morning. I lay there thinking, "I am very, very sorry but last night I shat all down your wall"? I don't think!!! Actually it was not as bad as that, as they had been aware during the night of some disruption and were understanding and sympathetic. I borrowed some plasterer's tools from Don, and am happy to report dear reader; that it came off virtually in one piece and languished in the back garden until the warmer weather obliterated it.

The time between then and the deadline for my departure passed in a bit of a fog, due to tiredness from the night's sickness. However absorbing the views of the immediate area, as well as planning in my mind the coming summers efforts with this "beautiful" pile of old stones captured most of my attention for the rest of that day.

It seemed no time at all that I was returning down the M5 towards Exeter, both nervous and elevated alternatively, bearing this news back to my family, there was no doubt as to where the summer holiday was to be spent this year! Our caravan would be situated on site in the garden; the two children would love it.

The news was received at home with great excitement, and thoughts of the great adventure ahead were captivating all the family. What a prospect!!!

3 - We Gain a Week (*and a Mum in Law*)

The humdrum of our lives and work dragged us back to reality for the next few months and apart from the "British Cheque in Francs" eventually explained and sorted at our bank. The arrival of some paperwork from France along with the odd letter from Don and Cher from the village was all there was to remind us of my winter excursion to those foothills of the Pyrenees.

I had started compiling a list of essential tools that would have to be taken with us and those that would have to be purchased down there.

Cement mixer, wheel barrow and heavy tools could not practically be taken in the car. My electrical tool list was very comprehensive already but careful planning of the initial work would reduce it a bit, but my thoughts about our arrival and the siting of the caravan would be the first priority. I felt to park it in the public square would be provocative and so to get it onto our own property very quickly would be diplomatic.

We knew that the mayor of the village Mr Fosse had a direct view as he lived at the other end of the square, and that he had not been in office when the renovation had been approved and apparently was not over enamoured as his family tomb was very close to the back wall of the cottage!

The garden, by the time we arrived would have had a season's growth of weeds and would not be in any condition to receive a car, caravan and awning. Don and Cher did not have a mower and besides were now so involved in their own project would not, I am sure, want to spend valuable summer time clearing what was now our garden. I had a good quality, but heavy self propelled mower here in England. Would we find room for it in the boot of the car? I decided it might be the last thing loaded so that it would be first out on arrival! Such detail, you may think, may seem unnecessary but after all it was "The end of the world" we were going to and had to be approached in that way.

Alex's mum (already a great Francophile) wondered if she could ride with us part of the way down to her own holiday home in the Dordogne as she planned to spend part of her summer there that year.

Here we were, trying to wedge all we wanted to take in our car and caravan, and now another body (substantial) might have to be considered! "No way" I said to Alex; "with the four of us and all that would be needed for the project, we would now need a lorry not a car to tow our caravan." Well as it turned out nothing is that simple.

Tacey would be coming down from Warwick University at the end of June and Jon's 'A' levels finished at the same time. Alex (primary school teacher) broke up in the third week of July. Another plan was forming in my mind! I could actually leave with Alex's mum, Tacey and Jon a week or two earlier and Alex could follow by coach later when school finished.

Her mother could be safely delivered, the caravan would be sited, and I would have gained at least a week or so on the project. Sorted!

So now we spent time discussing Alex's coach journey and searching for routes and times, and realised that it would be possible. The coach would arrive in Perpignan – a two hour drive from the village. A tough journey for her, but she could see the plus points and was prepared to take it on.

A date was decided between mum (in law) and the rest of us for the beginning of July and we duly booked a crossing with the ferry company. At that time Sealink's "Maid of Kent" sailed from Weymouth to Cherbourg. Now with this booked and confirmed, everyone had a sense of "here we go", but several more weeks of organisation were left before our departure, not least of which included sorting out the living expenses for the six weeks, but also for the cost of the travel.

No great investments were needed for the house project initially, but some cash would be needed for sand, cement and lime for building the walls, and some allowance made for the purchase of heavy tools and a bit more for providing a water heating boiler.

My list of essential tools had been carefully sifted through and rationalised. It would be necessary to buy a pick and shovel, but as I was much more adept using my own smaller hand tools, these would have to be loaded into the caravan under the bedding of the bunks before setting off. This list would be no doubt altered a little as the deadline neared.

Alex had the caravan equipment sorted out to suit her requirements, but decided that to take some basic foodstuffs including tinned food for “emergencies”. Perhaps her vision of what we might face was more practical than mine, but then I thought “what if?” in the event of car accident or breakdown and not being able to reprovision with fresh food for example? We were going to be some distance from any real civilisation, so we had to bear that in mind: All credit to her for the thought.

Mother in Law was delighted that we could now accommodate her for her trip to the Dordogne but also understood that there would be some restriction on what she could transport. For convenience she would sleep at our house the night before we left. The crossing being early afternoon a prompt start would be necessary on that day which was now approaching very quickly.

The weekend before leaving must be devoted to packing tools etc. into the caravan, as weight distribution for safe travel was very important. So the list had to be very carefully adhered to. Tacey and Jon had to sort out their clothes and anything else essential for their six weeks away, and amid all this seeming chaos, order was achieved as the long awaited morning arrived.

4 - Mum Safely Delivered

(And she had me in stitches!)

Alex's departure for school that morning, with the usual "Don't forget this" and "Don't forget that" having taken place, and with final kisses and "see you all in ten days time", all was now ready. She, who will now remain known as "Mum", had stayed the night and so with a final check and look around, doors were locked and we were off.

Weymouth next stop, and then on to the ferry; by later that evening we would be in Cherbourg and tomorrow down through France to the Dordogne to deliver Mum to her holiday cottage surrounded by fields of maize and sunflowers.

Not for us this very popular area, so similar to the Devon countryside. We were going much further through France to the Lauragaise region of the Aude department, where at that time there were hardly any British property owners (Don and Cher excepted) and only a few English visitors even during the height of summer. Channel Ferries were much too far away. The nearest airport was Toulouse, and the no frills air travel not yet invented.

The crossing was calm, and apart from the car being very low to drive up the ramp on to the ferry which was solved by all the family walking on, and a "I am not amused" from Mum when asked, but eventually all passed without much incident.

After docking at Cherbourg we drove to Bayeux in Normandy and stopped at a campsite there for the night. Jon was chief "bread searcher" next morning and he arrived back with the first days "French goodies" eaten, and enjoyed, and we were soon cleared ready to go.

Caravan legs up, caravan hitched and away to find a supermarket, already spotted across the road to top up with fuel for the journey to the Dordogne. The caravan though heavy, had been carefully loaded to maintain a good balance with just enough weight on the tow-hook to give maximum control with safety, and was beautifully stable to drive. So it was "steady as it goes" all that day, reaching Mum's cottage late that afternoon. A couple of stops on the way for a sandwich and comfort break when desperate!

None of us had seen Mum's cottage until then, it had only recently been brought back to a state of habitation and though small was perfectly adequate for a summer stay. We were all on a bit of a high and after a drink or two with our evening meal; Jon and I went to the caravan to search out our sleeping bags.

Typical of me, when he had the bunk lifted up, I couldn't resist nudging his backside with my toe so that he overbalanced and nose dived into the bunk. There were screams of laughter and Jon saying "I'll get you for that". One would have thought that I should have been too old for this sort of caper, but even in 'half maturity' (40's) I still, enjoyed a joke. Wearing floppy sandals and in fast retreat, I shot out of the caravan and catching the toe of one of them on the way, spread my length up some stone steps.

I lay there for a minute or two staring at the star filled sky as Jon asked me if I was alright, and not being quite sure, realised that a medical investigation would have to be made. Tacey and Mum arrived to find Jon trying to lift me up, with blood running down my leg from my left knee.

Somebody brought a white garden chair and a box of tissues and I sat for a while to gather myself. Mum (who was an ex-nurse) had a first aid box on site and after cleaning a very split knee, wrapped it up for that night which I spent awkwardly as it stiffened up with the bruising. Yes I know, we hadn't arrived yet and here I was having "crocked myself" fooling around.

With the morning came the realisation that it might be a little more than just a scratch; I was so stiff I could barely move, as my whole body was shaken up and with a leg I couldn't bend. Mum redressed the wound and in her most Matronly commanding manner pronounced "Michael this needs a couple of stitches, you may need an x-ray and although I don't think anything is broken I hope your tetanus injection is up to date".

Calamity!! "My mind was whirring, we were now going to continue our journey and with this injury would I even be able to drive? That question was answered quite quickly. Struggling to get behind the steering wheel; I found clutch work to be impossible.

Jon had passed his driving test the previous September and so he ferried me to the local doctor, who after careful examination, proceeded with four stitches. Then added that there was no breakage and, like mum, asked if my tetanus boost was up to date. My past history gave the answer to that and he understood the precautions that a farmer and builder/renovator would have taken.

When I mentioned driving he laughed and said he imagined, pointing at Jon that I had not driven to the surgery and should not expect to be able to bend it until the stitches came out in a week.

So, had the time we had gained been put in jeopardy by a bit of horseplay I wondered? Jon also had a pensive look on his face, and looked a bit worried. Okay, he was a young driver, but had plenty of practice on the farm driving tractors and trailers, so had experience with towing and reversing such things. He said he would give it some thought, which he did, bless him, and after our goodbyes to Mum, we left the Dordogne for our "second leg" in France. No pun intended! Tacey asked how long this would take and I said as long as your brother feels confident and before tiredness overtakes him.

Well, he did brilliantly and soon had the feel of the load and the way that the caravan assisted in braking each time he came to a halt. Driving around the outskirts of Toulouse obviously stretched his concentration and we were all pleased when we found ourselves on the link road "Entre Deux Mers" in the direction of Narbonne.

This passed through a heavily cultivated and fertile valley with acres of sunflowers, cereals and grapes. We were now truly in the far South West of France with the hills sloping up to the Pyrenees, dotted with small fields and groups of Cypress trees.

The roofs of the houses were now, of course, covered with red pantiles. We had been watching the colours of the tiles slowly change as we drove down through France; mostly of slate in Normandy, a mix as we moved down past the Loire valley and now all red and yellow in the south. Not only an indication of strata, I felt, but also signifying the rise in temperature.

Now and again as we travelled, we spotted the Canal du Midi running adjacent to the road which would lead us eventually to Castelnaudary. I can remember stopping by the side of that road for a sandwich and to stretch our legs. Though in my case it was only the one! Jon was visibly relaxing; he was now quite confident with his towing and both Tacey and I were totally relaxed with his ability.

So on to Castelnaudary, which was very different from the last time I was here: A twinge in the stomach as we drove past the restaurant where I had been fool enough to eat moules, on over the bridge of the canal and on to the seventeen kilometres of wandering roads back to the little village. We were excited now, and I was apprehensive at the reaction I would have from the two of them.

As we left Castelnaudary and started climbing, we were amazed to see huge bays of yellow flowering broom and the scent that was entering the car was heady, and to us evocative of previous hot summer holidays we had spent in the south.

Tacey thought this part of the country was reminiscent of Spain, and we speculated that as the other side of the not too distant border was Spain, it probably was very similar.

We passed through two very run down villages with the usual scruffy dog or two and the occasional furtive cat. Something else familiar to the south, it seems; 'Les vieilles grand-mères', dressed in black, carefully parked outside near the front step by their families. Dozing in the sun and in some cases, though not missing the passing of a stranger in a foreign car.

As we climbed slowly up towards the village the change in the countryside from that winter visit was more and more apparent. Transformed from that coat of white, to heat soaked browns and greens of the trees, which marked the most profound difference. Many of the summer crops had already been harvested, leaving yellow stubble in the fields and in many cases large round and square bales of straw, yet to be collected. The farm houses and buildings which were generally surrounded by Cypress trees were some considerable distances apart, suggesting arable farms of some size.

The odd small flock of sheep seemed to be confined to the scrubbier areas which were unfit for the plough and usually guarded by a shepherd (often Grandpa or Grandma and dog) but no cattle were in sight, perhaps they were housed for the summer.

5 - Reviewing the Site and Tacey in Shock.

So we crept through the lanes to the village and the memories of my last visit flooded back. Now in the midst of a hot summer it looked dusty and deserted. Tacey was staring at the square and the church with her mouth open, but Jon, bless him, said "Where to Dad?" I pointed to the end of the square and he slowly drove past the old Forge.

They both said "Surely not that Dad?" and I said "no, not that one" and I pointed to the ruin that I had bought which now seemed buried in weed and neglect. Some part of the front wall was visible, but the small courtyard and the garden (poetic licence) were buried in weeds six feet tall at least! Even my heart sank as we got out and examined the situation closer.

Both Tacey and Jon were aghast at the ruin and Tacey proceeded to get a chair from the caravan and take her book to the shade of the trees by the church. Her opinion of the whole situation obvious! They had both witnessed and lived with some of the challenges I had taken on in previous years, but they both thought that this was beyond the pale and obviously had doubts of my sanity!

Jon, looking at my leg and then at the "garden" said "What to do first?" so I replied "we unload the mower and cut our way into the garden – firstly, a line straight through the middle and then gradually work outwards to the boundaries. The caravan will have to wait here in the square on the level until we have a cleared an area in the garden to place it. Jon started to unload the mower from the back of the car (remember the planning?). I found the shears and started cutting a pathway to reach the installed water tap by the wall in the courtyard.

Later Tacey would make up a brew and then consider preparing something to eat, but as it was only just after four o'clock in the afternoon, we still had a few hours in which to complete this first stage.

The mower started without any problem and I demonstrated how to approach the jungle: Setting the blades high and propelling back and forward until approximately one metre was cut and clear, before attempting the next one. Jon was studying me with my stiff leg and said, "I'll do the first hour, and then you can have another go". I took the shears and started to cut and mark out the edge of the building and the line of the stone wall so that we could see the area we were working towards!

The bag of the mower filled very quickly, and an area adjacent was quickly identified for dumping the cuttings so we could clear the ground as we went. In no time the path was established. This had taken at least twenty minutes and it was not hard to realise that we would not get the caravan in that day, but the clearing was changing the look and size of the garden as each strip was finished, which spurred us on.

My leg had to be kept straight, but the general stiffness was easing with the exercise, and being able to share the effort with Jon was getting the job done more quickly.

Tacey was now somewhat resigned at what she considered to be a total disaster and was organising an evening meal consisting of cold meat and salad, tomatoes and bread, cold beer and/or wine and fruit – great! Don and Cher had heard the commotion and having let us descend from the ecstasy to disaster (in the words of Tacey) arrived to greet us but soon departed as they saw the amount of work going on to establish some order which was now beginning to take place. The caravan had been sited close to the front of the cottage, stabilised and jacked up for the night and we were sitting at the entrance of the garden enjoying a last glass of wine before a well deserved rest.

At least two thirds of the area had been cleared, and it was much bigger than any of us had realised. There would be plenty of room for a caravan and the car to be parked, the BBQ set up and with adequate space to work in when necessary!

Clearing the garden had already revealed the huge lengths of timber for the roof of the building which had been sheeted down and well protected. Inside the skeleton of the building could be seen, again well wrapped and covered, the doors, windows, toilets, wash bowls and pipe work etc. My enthusiasm was returning; it would be the great adventure I had envisaged.

Jon, because of his contribution seemed to be catching my mood, but Tacey, realising we were miles from anywhere, with no company or chance of meeting any, I sensed would be happier when her Mother (as opposed to Mum) arrived.

In the morning, after clearing the rest of the garden we discussed the siting of the caravan and then with jacks wound up, it was carefully reversed into place by Jon under my experienced guidance.

In the two far corners of the garden were fig trees which had died back as a consequence of the severe winter, and I noticed that bay trees around the village had suffered the same fate! I also noted, with much pleasure, piles of old and very usable stone lying against the left wall. Weathered old stone was a huge asset, and for the walls would give an aged and very satisfying finish.

Once the caravan awning was erected, the whole place started to look much more like the holiday and work site that I had imagined.

I slipped over to Don and Cher's to get directions to the supermarché, and also the whereabouts of a builders merchant in the town. I thought I had spotted one on the route on our side of Castelnaudary. We were going to need sand, cement and lime for the walls, and they would be required quite soon.

So after lunch we would 'launch forth' to provision up for the first week. Alex would be with us later in the second week and would take command but at lunch we did make a list of our initial needs.

6 - Finding our Bearings.

Don had confirmed that the location of the builder's merchants, enterprise Tangios, to be much where I had thought. Then Cher gave directions to the Mammouth supermarché and also two other 'must go to' shopping locations; Spanghero's for fresh meat, (a very familiar family name in French rugby, as two brothers had played for the national side), and an agricultural cooperative. This was superb for their freshly harvested melons, peaches, nectarines and other seasonal produce.

These outlets proved to offer all and more than we would need, but we decided to visit the builder's merchants first.

As we drove into their yard we noticed who we supposed was the loader (grunt) of the business, a rough, surly, dusty looking chap, badly in need of a shave and a haircut, who eyed this alien car with its foreign occupants with what looked like great suspicion.

Tacey at this stage had taken fright and totally refused to come to the office and help, saying that her level French of would be incomprehensible to them. No amount of reasoning would help and as 'grunt' seemed about to approach the car, Jon and I got out and pointing my finger we walked towards their bureau/office.

Inside we negotiated our way through piles of materials to get to the desk, to be greeted in a very broad southern accent by one of two girls, the other busy at her typewriter. She was asking how she could help and appeared to be very sympathetic as we showed her our list.

Cement was easy, lime; we now discovered was, for them, 'chalk' or chaux and sand we knew to be 'sable'. We said at this point we specified the location of our project and she produced a local map of the area and pointed her finger to the right spot.

Great progress! She pressed a button on the front desk and after a few minutes the door opened and the man from the yard entered. He looked enquiringly at the receptionist who gabbled "Papa, blah blah blah blah blah sable blah ciment et chaux". He nodded, smiled showing several gold teeth and shook hands with both of us.

He pointed at the door and again in this hugely broad southern accent said (I think) "Avec moi". Well, we followed on and were taken to the sand heaps, to choose which and how much, and then to the cement and chalk. Hand gestures along with school boy French seemed to work.

In the big store I had noticed something else – decent wheel barrows, buckets and what looked to me like a Cornish shovel. I went along this line pointing at what I needed and with school boy grunts indicated how much was required whilst he noted it all down on a jotter.

Fantastic result! Back to the office we all went, monsieur with his list to the bureau, which the girls quickly put in to an order and then monsieur was asking what sounded like conned! Jon and I looked at each other confused and then we both got it. He was asking when (quand) we both said it as one! "Oui, quand" he said again to which I replied with great amusement in my best new southern accent “Demeng!” or as most would recognise “demain”. He said “De bonne heure?” “Weh” (oui) I responded and all was decided.

Before I left I enquired about yellow sand, as all he had was of a normal slightly grey to white, and we were told to go to the yellow sand seller on the road to Mirepoix. Fine, we didn’t need a lot; it was for pointing stonework and for casting lintels and surrounds of doors and windows.

We left, well pleased with our efforts, having been told to pay” demeng meteng” and continued into town for provisions.

We soon had the back of the car loaded and had super melons and peaches, fresh vegetables, bread, wine and cold beer. Milk would have to be the long life variety, and we would need to get used to it.

The wine came in returnable deposit bottles and seemed to be a local vin de table of Minervois grown on the left side of the valley towards Carcassonne and Narbonne. As it seemed not much dearer than bottled water we would try it!

Whilst in the farm producers store I had found garden hose in rolls, and because we had to make some provision for bodily cleanliness, I bought two rolls. Standing at the garden tap to wash down and then a bowl for more private parts behind a half built wall hardly did the job; more improvisation was definitely needed.

7 - What a Shower we Turned Out to Be

The hose was connected to the tap and then unrolled around the garden perimeter and as there was a hundred metres of it, it went all the way round like a giant yellow snake. The rose of the watering can, purchased at the same time, was securely wired to the end of the hose and passed over a lower branch of an old plum tree in a secluded corner of the garden. Three posts were then erected and an awning ground sheet tied to them as a screen in order to give privacy. Lo and behold we had a shower, albeit that first night was decidedly chilly, but with the warmth of a day's sunshine playing on the hose we would then have a different result completely

Tacey and Jon elected to wash using the bowl that night, probably a good decision as some slats would be needed tomorrow to prevent a mud heap forming in our makeshift shower.

First thing the next morning we prepared an area for the sand we were expecting to be delivered and got all the weeds out from the front of the cottage. By 8:00 am we could hear a lorry labouring up the road towards the village. The driver saw us and drove over; gesticulating we pointed at the cleared area and after barrowing (wow good barrow) the bags of cement and lime inside the building, he tipped the sand in a tidy heap just where we needed it.

The bill with the weight of sand (with the delivery docket attached) was duly paid by cheque and the driver drew away with a wave. Now things were getting organised!

The next chore, however, was to make the slatted duck board for our shower floor. Batons that we would use for this were tied in bundles for the roof work, many more than would be needed and so ideal for our duck board. Four slats long ways, four on the diagonal, nailed together, dig two narrow trenches about four inches deep to take away the water, lay the slatted floor over them and bingo, we had a shower for tonight.

Having a coffee in hand we all gazed and wondered what the result would be. More of that later in the day!

The planning permission drawing showed an extension from the old cottage continuing out into the garden, narrowing as it went. It used the cemetery wall on one side and an old existing wall to the courtyard on the other. This roof would be pitched left to right, to a gutter bringing rain water back into a soak-away at the bottom of our garden.

On the courtyard side there was to be a door and a window to gain light for the kitchen and for the downstairs bathroom. Internally, a new wall would enclose this bathroom with a door to the hall. We hoped to have this structure roofed in by the end of this year's work.

Whilst clearing the weeds at the foot of the inner walls of the extension we had disturbed two adders, one of which suffered instant death as the shovel descended on its head with some considerable force, whilst the other escaped into the garden wall half way down towards the corner. Knowing that they would not pass through builder's lime I spread a little from there to the beginning of the floor of the building and after that had no more sightings of them – much to everybody's relief.

Jon started to get a mix of cement together whilst I began sorting some stones. Large good finished pieces in one heap, small good faces in the second heap and nondescript/rubble in the third. I have found that there is no quicker way with old stone than to have a keen eye.

With experience in building natural stone walls I have learnt that it is not always a good idea to be too picky about selecting stones of the same size as it is this variation that gives the structure a beautiful random look, as well as making it incredibly strong. I soon had three tidy heaps, and it was as I had initially thought; the aged colours were superb and the occasional change caused by fire had added to the melange.

As Jon had now "knocked up" our first mix of sand and lime cement, we were soon loading and barrowing it along with the stones to the first part of the wall backing on to the cemetery.

Jon remarked that with the amounts of cement obviously needed, would not a small cement mixer be necessary to speed up the operation. I agreed and said that some sort of platform or scaffold would be essential for the higher right hand wall and so a further visit to town would be necessary. We would also need concrete blocks for the bathroom wall; so the size and number would have to be calculated for a future delivery. For the lower wall that we had started, two strong trestles with two of the heavier roof timbers placed on them would suffice.

Tacey seemed more relaxed now and was producing coffee when needed and food, gaining the beginnings of a good tan and reading – no doubt counting the days to the time when her mother would join us.

This being now Thursday, and Alex would be arriving in Perpignan next Tuesday at 1 PM and Tacey would prepare sandwiches for a picnic lunch on our way back.

So back to the present; it would be sensible to do something about a cement mixer and a scaffold before then and make a second order to the builders merchants, the blocks for the bathroom wall, more cement, lime etc. "That can wait until tomorrow or Monday" I said; Jon immediately piped up "Doesn't everything close on a Monday dad?".

This was something that we had come to realise on all our journeys through France over the years, though not without being caught out on a couple of occasions. We decided to do it on the Friday then and to make sure that we checked their opening hours whilst there.

The progress on the raising of the cemetery wall continued for the rest of the day and we eventually arrived at the decision of "Who showers first?" – Actually neither of us would be first. That crafty Tacey had Jon tend to the tap earlier in the afternoon and she advised us to be careful as the pipe lying in the sun meant that the water was quite hot. So I then opted to have my shower and Jon once again manned the tap.

The water was indeed quite hot and I quickly soaped up and flannelled off, shouting to Jon to switch off the water as I had finished. I towelled down, slipped on pants and shorts hanging conveniently on the plum tree and said "Right Jon, your turn now – take care it is still hot! I'll man the tap for you..."

Very soon he shouted "OK" and we had gauged that half a turn on the tap would provide sufficient pressure, he shouted "Fine" and then "Yes it is fairly hot", followed by "No, that's great", and then a shriek and "Shut the f**king thing off!!!". All the heated water had been used up and it had suddenly started running water on direct mains temperature – a sudden change of over 20° C. After turning off the tap, Tacey and I were gripping our sides laughing and Jon, although seeing the funny side, said "Your turn last tomorrow Father!"

That evening, after eating, Don and Cher dropped over to see how we were doing and were mightily impressed at what we had already achieved. They said that the volumes of hilarity they could hear had prompted their visit and Jon showed them the object of the mirth. They told us that they had managed with something similar in the past, but it had not been so sophisticated as having drainage and a slatted floor; more laughter followed as we gave them Jon's reaction to the rush of cold water!

8 - Bad News from the Mairie

(Ending in Thunder!)

We watched the evening sun go down over the undulating hills and then start to disappear behind the Pyrenees; it really is a beautiful part of the south and so unspoilt by change – apart from the mechanisation of agriculture.

The fly catching birds were by now extremely busy – swifts, swallows and house martins all had colonies under the eaves of, and inside the old forge. As it darkened, these were replaced by a great number of bats, the old buildings and the forge roof offering large areas of comfort for them as well, although I did wonder how many of them had died in that horrible past winter. Sleep was difficult that night, the air seeming lifeless and heavy, but eventually I drifted into slumber.

Friday morning and the stitches in the knee had to come out, and as I had only four, I decided to remove these myself, and as I had redressed and kept it 'plastered' (changing it each evening), it had healed well. I was looking forward to be able to start bending it, as our activities now were increasing to include heavier work! Nail scissors and needle nosed pliers soon completed the task, and a plaster to prevent dust and muck entering was applied to allow a little more healing time, and by the Monday it should be as good as new. Jon assisted with the bottom two stitches, as I couldn't quite see them; I felt that all would be well with it by the time Alex arrived.

So once more off to town with Jon, for us to find and purchase a small cement mixer and also to see if we could source some sort of scaffolding; we would stop at Tangio's first with our new order for concrete blocks, and then go on to Mr. Bricolage further down the road to search for the cement mixer and scaffolding. Don had mentioned that there was a Catena at Mirepoix which we would explore at a later date but it was further to travel.

We were greeted by many smiles by the daughters at the merchants and agreed to order a palette of mixed cement and lime plus blocks which they would send out on the light truck. No cement mixers or scaffold, sadly, but try the Brico down the road, which had a lot of material on show outside the front of the store, amongst which was a sixteen rung aluminium extension ladder which also could be clipped into a pair of very useful steps.

There was a cement mixer, and a very French (and by this I mean complicated) small scaffold with platform - not, perfect by any means, but would probably do the job. An assistant arrived and we pointed out the items we wanted, and asked if we could get all of this in or on our large estate car. He pointed to the tailgate and gave a sign indicating to put the back seats down, and said “weh” also indicating the roof rack. As it turned out both scaffold and cement mixer came boxed in an almost flat pack nature and loaded relatively easily. With the longer poles and ladder tied to the roof rack we made our way, slowly, back to the village.

We had coffee before unloading, and commencing with the cement mixer, started assembling our purchases together. No stress, practical and not too heavy, the cement mixer was soon in place. Jon was sorting plugs and adaptors to connect it to the existing electricity box on the wall in the skeleton of the building.

I decided it would be best to build and erect the scaffold in the area where the doorway would be cut through the existing wall into the courtyard. One could then take the stones out of the wall from the top down thus avoiding any possible collapse.

Having erected the scaffold we stood back to assess it. Yep very French: Intricate with a narrow hinged flap/trapdoor to access the platform and with outriggers for stability. The instructions said that it should only be used by one operative at a time, which we didn’t doubt given it’s apparent fragility. It looked cheap (which it was), but also looked as though it might serve our purpose.

Jon's delight was the cement mixer; simple in design and with a 1½ HP electric motor to give plenty of power to a barrel that would deliver a barrow of mix at each feeding. Now well equipped, the work would proceed apace and we lunched and looked forward to a good afternoon's progress. Little did I know!

After lunch Don and Cher arrived and produced a letter from our local mayor (he who lived at the other end of the square) which informed us that he now opposed the project to renovate the cottage, as it had passed over into new management (meaning us). We stood totally shocked and discussed whether he (as mayor) had the power to do this or not. We were aware that Mayors in France had much more clout than in England and remembered that European rulings counted for little, as he was quoting the ancient Napoleonic code. The regional planning committee sat at Bram, a small town nearer to Carcassonne and it was decided that Cher would ring that office to arrange a meeting later in the week with someone much better qualified to advise us and so that Alex could be with me to lend her support for this crisis! After they had departed we sat completely deflated and Tacey said "What on earth are you going to do now?" Having given it a little thought, I said "Well I think the answer is to stop building upwards, and start taking down the wall for the doorway and the window of the bathroom.

When that was finished, as we had the blocks we could continue with the bathroom wall and internal door, removing the emphasis for the moment from the proximity of the churchyard which would appear to be the reason for his objection.

So we continued, but not with quite so much enthusiasm as before. Jon would have preferred to make much more noise with the cement mixer and shovel, so that Mr. Le Mayor would think that his authority had no impact on us, but my decision was a little more diplomatic and quieter!

We were working as a team and having marked the outline for the door on the wall, we started to remove the stone from this area using a stone chisel. Jon passed the stones one at a time to me, and as before I was grading them into their respective piles. The rubbish and rubble was brushed off from the stones and into the courtyard and could be cleared later.

As the old wall had not much ‘bind’ to it, progress was swiftly made, apart from the occasional very large stone that overlapped into what was to remain of the wall. If by deep marking with a chisel it could be cracked off, fine; undermining it usually achieved this result, but if the stone had to come out and leave a wider aperture than desired, this could easily be rectified later!

As we worked the mayor was very much on our minds and occasionally Jon (when giving a stone a mighty blow) would bellow “Fosse!!!” (The mayors name) which Tacey and I thought was a step too far, but really quite amusing. So he desisted and the doorway slowly appeared and as it was two and a half feet wide, a lot of good stone was now stacked behind me. We were both covered in dust and after brushing up and pulling the scaffolding away we reached the bottom part of the doorway.

Time to stop for a shower: “Me first!” Jon quickly reminded me!

When Alex arrived a proper schedule for the shower would have to be implemented, starting earlier in the day. Tacey had again had hers earlier in the afternoon giving the sun time to do its work. So, once more to the tap and all went well. Jon had a quick shower and the water was soon switched off again, and in a few minutes he was ‘shorted’ and ready to man the tap for me.

Clean shorts and towel on plum tree, strip off and toss dirty clothes over the curtain and a shout of “OK” was all that was needed to start my shower. Lovely, all was going well and with the last of the soap nearly all rinsed off the ice cold water arrived. I shouted “Off!!!” the rose head spluttered, and then blew off the end of the hose! A huge gush of really freezing water doused me.

I shot out of the shower, wet yes, no soap yes, but cold and stark bollock naked! My dry clothes were sodden. Jon, it seemed, had put the tap on full blast as soon as he had heard me shout “Off” which of course had blown off the shower head. Pay back for laughing at him yesterday and both Jon and Tacey were killing themselves with mirth. I found some other clothes to wear for the evening and hung out the wet ones to dry.

The evening was, again, very hot and heavy and we agreed that a thunderstorm could arrive that night, and so due care was taken to secure coverings over materials, check car windows and awning pegs and generally make preparations.

Later, after our BBQ, heavy storm heads were appearing from the direction of the Pyrenees; teasing gusts of wind were already eddying around and about, causing dust to swirl in the square and the open awning to flap. Darkness came early that night with the imminent arrival of the storm and we were to experience the first of many that this corner of France is accustomed to, and which are caused by the extreme summer heat of the area and the proximity of the mountains.

The storm arrived and performed a veritable symphony with added pyrotechnics due to the lightning (mostly sheet) coming at all angles and then the thunder, finishing with a growl and on many occasions a huge clap. The three of us could only watch and wonder at the display of this raw natural power.

Very soon after, the rain came and so we dashed into the awning and then into the caravan as the sky just emptied. It was torrential and we sat there with the storm still raging and the lightning giving an eerie look to the cottage, church, square and village outside.

The morning broke clear and bright; coming out of the caravan the change from yesterday was remarkable, the first thing that struck me was the smell. It was the fresh clean smell of renewal; the heat soaked ground, vegetation and even stone all giving off that distinctive freshness that only comes after rain falls on parched ground.

Visually, everything looked sharper, as even the air had been cleansed of all the dust and pollen. There is always a musty, almost antique smell to recovered stone, which had been changed this morning due to the natural washing by the rain, but still not having a newly quarried smell. I strolled up to the square and found that it too looked refreshed and a different smell was rising from the tarmac, which was already starting to steam as it dried in the sun The swifts, swallows and house martins were flying high searching for their breakfasts and calling excitedly to one another. I turned back to the caravan to join them in their quest for sustenance! It had the promise of a beautiful day with the heaviness of the last few days having departed with the storm.

As we ate we chatted about the extremes of the thunder and lightning. The storm had passed over around midnight but seemed to come back for a short encore about two hours later after which we must all have fallen into a deep slumber which meant we felt rested for another day.

We were to continue with yesterday's effort and then move on to the window and possibly the walls of the bathroom. Jon enquired whether we would be permitted to continue, and I said "I don't know, but that we needed to take a positive view until proven differently", meaning that we would not proceed with any external wall building for the time being.

Tomorrow (Sunday) we would keep a low profile, no doubt there would be a church service and perhaps relatives bringing flowers to their forebears resting in the churchyard just over our wall. Perhaps Mr Le Mayor would be attempting to drum up support on the Sabbath for his objection to our project – who knows, but a little bit of diplomacy could not hurt our cause. So, Sunday is closed.

Today, however, we got on with the bathroom window, the size (height and width) including the sill had been marked out, remembering that all windows in France open inwards – meaning the sill couldn't be used as a shelf.

On examining the window frame already provided, we discovered that it had flap openings at the top to allow air circulation and was already pre-glazed with opaque glass. So perhaps we *would* be able to reclaim the sill as a shelf after all. Jon started removing stones and once again I was sorting and stacking, but this time in the courtyard; we needed to keep the floor clear in the interior for the work of constructing the new bathroom wall and door.

That work was scheduled for the following week and would probably occur after Alex arrived. Don, bless him, ambled over with two casting boxes for pillars and lintels that would work for doorways and windows.

The boxes each came with two separators and a batten which went in the bottom so that each block would have a recess for fitting the shutters. Simple but brilliant, as each could be tailored to any length desired and with steel embedded, would give support to the wall building above, and on this cottage they would vary window to window. The arrival of these boxes reinforced our need for yellow sand, and reminded us that we would have to get some the following week. White cement and yellow sand when mixed together would cast a block that strongly resembled the colour of the natural stone of that area and they would look the business! Of course, one could buy cut yellow sandstone which would look spectacular, but having checked the price, realised that this was an unnecessary expense when we could fabricate something ourselves that certainly would have the same look and feel. This was practical and economic and suited my Cornish farmer outlook and pocket. Brushing the sides of the casting boxes with a little diesel fuel should prevent the mix from sticking, whilst putting them to set in the shade would also prevent them from drying too fast – good advice from Don, we didn't want ones with cracks in them! The sides of the casting boxes unscrewed which also meant there would be no "whacking" to free the blocks, again preventing the risk of damaging them.

The weekend weather, after the storm, was beautiful and temperatures were certainly starting to climb. In the square we had an old public telephone box and eventually we were all able to have a few quick words with Alex to wish her a "bon voyage" for her imminent bus journey through France and give her a little briefing of how we had progressed, but as Jon aptly put it "Don't mention the war" – meaning the dispute with the mayor; there would be more than enough time for that once she arrived.

9 - All About the Smallest Room

After preparing the opening for the window, we slowly sorted through the bathroom fittings. We thought that installing the internal wall and door, it would be very sensible to place the porcelains into position first.

Drainage for the house was in place under the floor and there was already a fosse septic (septic tank) buried in the garden which would prove to be important for us at this stage. This meant that the toilet could now be placed and its waste pipe joined, to mark the first trappings of domestication on site for the family. In the meanwhile we had been using the chemical toilet in the caravan and when it was full, emptying it into the fosse. I wouldn't miss that chore, and the building of the wall inside would give us the luxury to perform absolutely in private! At this point we were reminded of Cher's taste as all the toilet covers were in bright primary colours!

The internal door for the bathroom was complete with its frame and was already supplied with handles, locks and hinges, and could be built right into the block work as the wall went up. The shower would back on to the kitchen wall so the plumbing for that could pass through the wall, keeping the water supply conveniently close together – which would be of enormous help.

The hot water was to be provided by a large electric boiler which would be placed in an alcove on the other side of the hall/bathroom wall, centrally situated, making the water also equally accessible for the plumbing to the second floor of the cottage. I knew with my renovating experience that thinking the 'long game' with a bit of forward planning now would save so much time later on.

Jon and I admired the placing of the bathroom furniture, because even though there was still a lot to do, one could really get a mental picture of how it would look, and we called Tacey to come and see. She stared, and no surprise to either of us, said “If you think I’m going to use any of that as it is, you’ve another thought coming. No way, not in a month of Sundays”. Jon and I burst out laughing as she flounced off, “girls of that age are so conscious of their bodies” I remarked and Jon said “Yep I can be quite conscious of the bodies of girls of that age too – but obviously not that of my sister!”

Flooring was playing on my mind and I already had the address and directions for a wood yard on the outskirts of Castelnaudary on the motorway side of town. Floor boarding and I mean properly prepared timber from local pine was available. Tongue and groove, no less, but with some knots and quite resinous; one was advised to get each pack of 10 x 240 x 20cm laid and nailed quickly into place, as they would start to warp as soon as the cords were cut if stored out in the sun.

Their timber supplies would not be something that a British builder would easily understand: No prepared skirting boards, architraves or generally finished timber was available. Carpenters generally bought their lumber in bulk, and as most of them had their own workshops with electrical operated benches for preparing what they needed. I had electric saws, one large and one small, as well as a heavy duty electric plane, so we could improvise the skirting boards and as the doors had been provided with frames, I could not see much of a problem there.

Alex would be bringing some more Francs with her (this was in the pre-Euro epoch) to help with additional needs. We had a French bank account with the Banque Nationale de Paris in Castelnaudary that we had already deposited funds into over the previous months. That ought to be sufficient for most day to day expenses, and her cash would be used for food and day to day supplies.

A bakers van pulled into the square twice a week and a local fruit grower with fantastic peaches called maybe twice a month. They were freshly picked and had the most amazing flavour; they were so ripe that it was impossible to eat them without getting juice all down ones chin! “Gosh!” I had remarked to Tacey and Jon, “Your mother won’t half enjoy these!”

Marking the floor for the interior walls with a straight edge (an aluminium plank about 4 metres long), with chalk was a simple job, especially as now everything was already in place. Building the wall in a traditional manner meant that corners and doorways were started first and the gaps between filled in as you went.

This provides a good solid framework, especially as cuts had to be made into the two existing walls to tie the new into the old. The corners are interwoven for maximum strength – it is surprising quite how much stress can be applied to a wall when a door slams because of a draught coming through an open window and because of the peculiarities of French drainage; we suspected the bathroom window would be open quite a lot!

Well, as Sunday dawned, no surprise – there was no church service; a couple of ancients did come with flowers though, casting curious eyes in our direction, only to receive a bright "Bonjour!" in return. Since we had already decided that we wouldn't be working on Sunday we planned out our day...

I would have to estimate the square meterage of flooring we would need for the single story extension where the kitchen/dining area, hallway and bathroom were, so we would know how much tongue in groove to order when Jon and I visited the timber yard on Monday. It would be much easier to work this out now with no walls, kitchen units or bathroom fittings installed. Probably a dozen bundles, but the weight would have to be within limits for the estate car.

10 - Time Out and Then Back to Work

We decided a little exploration of Castelnaudary might be the order of the day as we had only seen a little of the town so far on our visits to the various suppliers, and thought that a walk beside the canal, with some research of restaurant menus would be just the ticket. We strolled along the towpath watching the bustle and movement of boats at the "Bassin" (marina) where some were waiting their turn to move through the locks.

The Canal du Midi draws a lot of visitors, both on and off the water; holiday makers and water travellers both, meaning increased seasonal traffic and so the town was really starting to wake up. We located a café bar and sat at a table in the shade under their trees, overlooking the square; and over beers, coffee and a light lunch discussed the 'bird problem'.

The plane trees that were shading one side of the square had been inhabited by hoards of starlings who were doing a very good job in making sure that the area, and the cars of any foolish enough to park there, were plastered with their plentiful droppings. I wondered if, and how, the traders and city fathers might be tackling this problem as it must be having a dire effect on trade.

After a final tour of the square and a few of the streets beyond, taking notes of things that might be interesting to do or see on another occasion before returning to The village for a quiet evening; in fact, after our meal we all read a few chapters of our books and turned in soon after 10:00 PM.

Monday morning we were all up bright and early, and after pulling on shorts, putting a kettle on to boil, for a cup or mug of tea and then out to get a bowl of water from the tap. There was a glorious sky and not a soul in evidence; the only sounds to be heard were that of our fly-catching friends swooping and diving overhead. Taking a deep breath of satisfaction with my lot I poured the contents of the now boiled kettle into my mug containing a solitary teabag, the rest into my water bowl for a quick wash and shave.

"All is right with the world" I thought "and Alex would be with us tomorrow. Apart from the one downer I reminded myself as I heard a shutter clatter back as it was opened at the Mayor's house and glanced up through the square towards its source. I prayed that things would go right with that situation this week; it was quite obvious that the proximity of our activities to his family tomb was the reason for his action.

Tacey and Jon had now stirred and I put the kettle back on for our coffee and searched out bread, butter, jam and marmalade, which with a basket of fruit would make an excellent breakfast. Physical work makes one very hungry and although the long life UHT milk of the day was an acquired taste, Jon and I commenced with a large bowl of cereal. We needed to get the calories in if we were to get out the maximum effort – especially in that heat! It certainly seemed to be true that only mad dogs and Englishmen go out in the Aude in the Midday sun, something Cher had earlier remarked upon.

Tomorrow, I suggested, we may, and only may, be able to place our bums (old Cornish word) on a proper toilet. Jon seemed pleased with this, "great" he said, but Tacey realising that there was still no roof over it, looked a little doubtful. Leaving her to clear the table Jon and I soon departed for the wood yard. We saw only two other vehicles on the Route Nationale to Castelnaudary, and only a few more as we drifted down into the town. The smell of the yellow flowered and spiny broom was filling the air with its cloying, sticky sweet scent drawn out by the warmth of the sun. This was now becoming so familiar to us even though we had been there only a short spell so far this year.

As we passed through the town, we noticed signs of life as people 'busied up' for the day. I took note of a barber's shop which was obvious by its traditional red and white pole as we passed, because I would need to have a haircut in this heat, and it would certainly hold less dust thus helping to cut down the time to shower.

"Quite a lot of Legionnaires around this morning", said Jon as we passed through, I agreed, some black, some white, some khaki; we discussed the nature of the French Foreign Legion, Jon speculating that it was a mercenary force made up of thugs, jail birds and misfits from all parts of the world, with most of the officers coming from Germany. "Some of that may be true" I said, "Films do tend to exaggerate the facts to the point where it becomes fiction, but I would think that there is no doubt that there are some here with very complicated backgrounds.

We soon found the wood yard and with the sounds of their saws ringing in our ears we went into their office. A helpful young man greeted us and as we looked down we saw that the floor was laid with just what we wanted to order, which with our limited French was immediately a great help to us. He asked us how much we required and I passed him my calculations with a cheerful "Combieng?" he wrote down the price per metre and with his calculator was able to quickly give a total for the order.

It was approximately half what I had expected, but of course as France has a huge wealth of timber in their "*Forêts* anciennes" this reduced its price. He then asked us to follow him into a large building adjacent to the office. Huge piles of timber were stacked here including beams and planks of all sizes, but set to one side were floor boards wrapped ten to a bundle. We would need a dozen bundles so I sent Jon to bring the car around and with the back seats down we quickly loaded what we needed, and after paying were soon trundling back through town.

I also needed a large plastic bowl and another bucket, so a quick stop at Bricolage was in order before once more taking the road to The village. I was delighted with our purchases, as I had even managed to find the headless nails we needed for fixing the floorboards. So we had plenty to do!

After a late coffee, we cut the frame of the bathroom door to fit the opening for height, not forgetting to leave half a centimetre above floorboard level for clearance. Being in France, I was being forced into using metric measurements when sizing materials for perhaps the first time in my life, which was not too much of a problem. What really puzzled me, however, was why continental plumbing used imperial measurements for taps and fittings, but metric for pipes!

After more than 20 years out here it still remains a mystery, not only to me, but all the other British expats who have lived here at some time or another.

The work in the bathroom would commence with the erection of the wall, building the door frame into it, and later, after the roof was on, we would lay the floor in the hall from the top step of the two leading down to the kitchen and dining room, and continuing, including the bathroom, as we progressed.

The window had not yet been finished (as we had yet to source the yellow sand) but this work of making the lintels could be done outside in the courtyard so as to prevent too much dust and rubble falling on the new floor.

So one mix of cement please Jon! We wheeled our mixer inside so the noise it made would be dampened by both the courtyard wall and also by the corner of the massive Old Forge on the other side of the lane, so as to mask it from "you know who". A mix was made, and then Jon held the bathroom door complete with frame exactly where we wanted it to be so that the first two blocks could be laid in tight on both sides. He then lifted the whole thing carefully aside so that we could start in the first corner by the kitchen, when these had been laid; we then filled the gaps between them.

In total the bathroom wall was going to have three corners, two that would be tied into the existing stone walls and an internal one where the kitchen wall turned 90°. This became the wall forming a corridor/hall to the upper part of the old building and it was that wall into which the door was placed, providing access to the bathroom. I measured carefully so that I could tell Jon what cut blocks I would need, for he had the precision job of deeply marking the blocks with bolster and lump hammer. After giving them a final sharp smack of the hammer the blocks split along the lines he had marked and after handing them to me I set them into cement along the first course.

This first course of blocks takes more time than any other to lay, so once it was finished we progressed more quickly. Jon soon caught on and was checking to see whether any of the ends of the blocks he had already cut could be used up as we went along. I said we should probably insert the door after the second course of blocks were in and he would be able to drill holes in the frame so that the anchor fixings could be built into the cement layers between the blocks.

Permanent placing of the door required us to make sure that it was both perfectly level and upright, meaning not only would we have to secure it like that to begin with, but that we would have to continue to monitor this as the walls went up. After checking with a spirit level, two batons were temporarily pinned to the top of the frame and across to the courtyard wall and weighted to be secure. Of course the proof would be in the pudding, if we had done this properly it would be proven by a door that swings correctly!

Four courses of blocks would be my maximum, any more than that and the additional weight on the wet cement risked damaging or toppling the work we had already done, more would be added on another day. As Alex would be arriving tomorrow, I knew that the cement would have plenty of time to set before we recommenced later in the week, and probably after our visit to Bram!

So much would hinge on the results of that meeting, and being a great cynic, I began to wonder about the connection between our burnt out ruin and the situation we had found ourselves in; had the cottage in fact been destroyed by arson?

We enquired from Tacey if there was anything that we could do to help before Alex arrived, but she was quite organised as ever, and said that no doubt they would go off together for a big stock up after she arrived and had assessed our needs. I felt sure that Alex would be pleased by the sleeping arrangements that we had adopted since we had arrived, because apart from the night of the storm, Tacey had been sleeping on a "put me up" cot in the awning which had not only given us more space in the caravan, but it was a lot more convenient than having to erect a second bunk every evening and putting it away every morning.

As for our ablutions, we would soon be able to use the toilet in the bathroom – even if it meant flushing it by filling the cistern with a bucketful of water, it would still be better than a chemical toilet and nearer to the caravan than the public loo in the square.

The car needed fuel, so a short diversion to the supermarket in the morning would be required before proceeding on to Perpignan. I decided that the day would be totally devoted to Alex, who would be anxious to see everything and hear all our news. I had no fear about her reaction in seeing what we had purchased; she had a different vision on these wrecks than Tacey and she would realise the potential of the project, just as I had.

She would have to face up to the mayor's objection as I was, and prayed all would be well by the end of the week. The whole family would go to meet her, as we were all excited that she would finally be there with us the following day, so we ate and then turned in early knowing that we would have a prompt start in the morning.

11 - Alex Arrives in Perpignan

After a hurried breakfast we were soon in the car and on the road out of the village, as we passed the mayor's house Jon (of course) started blowing raspberries which caused Tacey and I to have to stifle several guffaws. For Jon this was an indication of his love for *Monty Python and the Holy Grail*, which most will know had a scene where a French "kinigit" fires a stream of inventive insults at those below. So appropriate!

We fuelled the car at Castelnaudary and were soon on the route heading in the direction of Carcassonne, we would have to turn right at Narbonne to proceed to Perpignan. We noted the signposts to Bram, which was perhaps 20 km down the road, and marked it for our future visit at the end of the week.

Several tens of kilometres later the old medieval city of Carcassonne could be seen off to the left, we had visited here in the past but Tacey said it would be good for a trip, perhaps on a Sunday, and spend a little more time exploring it.

A little further down the road we passed the amazing symbolic stone sculpture of a group of "Knights" high on the causse and before long we were turning off towards Perpignan.

We now found more traffic as we joined the autoroute used by those travelling from Northern France along the south coast and into Spain.

Given the time of year, this meant it was a very busy stretch of road, and I would be pleased to see the turnoff to our destination which was some 85 km away.

Driving this section of road with so many lorries and tourist traffic wasn't pleasant, but at least the weather was good; just imagine how bad it could have been in inclement weather!

Although we were turning off at Perpignan, this road eventually curves its way round to the frontier town of Jonquera, popular for all its duty free shops. These days though, the main dual carriageway takes a slightly higher route to divert much of the heavier transport directly into Spain.

Much of the soft fruit and vegetables come up from that side of the country explaining the scores of refrigerated vehicles ploughing, as if in convoy, up and down the motorway.

Through the years, this coastal part of France, which is dotted with many fishing ports and shell fish farms, has been a great favourite of our family, and attracts a huge amount of visitors.

We arrived at Perpignan, and after locating the bus station, realised that we would have some time to wait before the coach from London would pull in, that is if it was on time. The journey that Alex would have taken was long, arduous and convoluted: A family friend had taxied her from our village on the Cornwall/Devon border to Exeter for the first leg of her voyage, then from Exeter to London Paddington by train, round the underground to Victoria Coach Station to catch a Eurolines' coach to Perpignan and all points South.

The coach was a two driver affair and stopped at several points through France not only to pick up and drop off passengers, but so the drivers could swap places, for rest breaks, and although they might get some sleep, I knew that it would be unlikely that Alex would because unlike me she never had the ability to catnap.

At last the coach swung around the corner and after a scramble for cases, she was with us: Tired, cramped and worn out, but able to give us all a big hug and kiss with the relief of a journey's end!

We piled into the car to head back towards The village. Everybody was speaking and laughing together, and after Alex "The School Teacher" had called order, we decided to stop at the first "aire" on the road heading back to Carcassonne.

We had fresh bread, butter, sliced ham and plenty of fruit, with bottled water to wash it down. Tacey had prepared and bagged some salad, and with paper plates we were well equipped for a continental picnic deep in the South of France under the shadow of the rising ground which is the Pyrenees, the natural border between France and Spain.

During this break I outlined what had happened with the mayor of the village and the letter received by Don and Cher. Her reaction was much like mine; shock, horror and then reason. I explained about the meeting that had been organised, and resignedly she agreed that we could do nothing else but see it through.

We then discussed the progression of work, according to our schedule, on the cottage and she was surprised to hear how much we had already achieved. I explained our act of diplomacy on Sunday and the decision not to work on the cemetery wall for the time being until the general situation re: planning became clearer.

Alex agreed that the proximity of the Fosse Family tomb to the cottage and cemetery wall almost certainly was the "crux of the matter", and that the current mayor had probably objected to the actions of the previous one when the planning permission had been granted.

Alex had seen nothing of Castelnaudary at this point so we gave her the guided tour and we were all pointing out one feature or another as we meandered our way through the town. We pointed out the problems in the central square of town caused by the roosting starlings and for some reason this reminded me of the rugby song "*Lighthouse in Mobile. Being a white house in Mobile*".

The presence of the French Foreign Legion was very evident today, as there were many uniformed personnel about, being policed by severe looking red caps who were keeping an eye on their off duty behaviour: Obviously very military and very controlled.

We passed the *Canal du Midi* and crossed over the bridge close to the marina (Bassin), and indicated the location of both the Mammouth supermarket and Spanghero, the butcher's depot explaining their usefulness to us, as we passed them. Further on there was the agricultural college, Mr. Bricolage and our friendly builders merchants. After crossing the bridge over the dual carriageway, we slowed down and opened the windows of the car so that Alex could appreciate the perfume of the huge bays of the yellow flowered broom decorating and bordering both sides of the road.

This area is known locally as the *Lauragaise* and is marked by having lots of small hills, many with villages or towns on them, and arable farms mostly growing barley and sunflowers; it was a very sleepy part of France we had both admired in years past.

It is also referred to as the Pays du Pastel as it was used for growing wode the wealth for many of the magnificent mansions seen around Toulouse were created through the wealth of this product but as it fell out of fashion with the arrival of indigo from India. It is also a region of the Vent d'Autan (The Autan Wind), which arrives from the south west, bringing with it the spicy red dust and heat from Africa.

Soon enough we arrived back at the village, and as we passed the Mayor's house Alex got the first glimpse of our ruin. There was no drama, in fact there was not much reaction at all – just concentration as she took in every little detail and absorbed the challenge we had taken on.

We drove in to the parking space in the garden and scrambled out anxious to see what the reaction might be once she had toured the whole site and assessed for herself the progress we had made.

In various stages her reaction was curiosity, amazement, excitement and enthusiasm about the property we had purchased and what we had already achieved, it took a full hour of investigation as we toured every inch of the project and its immediate surroundings, including the Old Forge and the cemetery, as Alex wanted to see the "tomb of contention".

It was the reaction I had hoped and expected to see, but I was relieved nonetheless; the undergrowth and mess we had cleared made the shell of the cottage look more like "work in progress" rather than the total wreck and ruin it appeared to be when we first arrived a little over a week before.

Travelling can be tiring and Alex was exhausted, so after a customary cup of tea, she went for a lie down for an hour or two before unpacking and having a shower to freshen up. As we were still using the makeshift shower, I made sure that I was the one manning the tap so that it went without a hitch!

She donned holiday clothes, and I could sense the stresses of a long term of boisterous youngsters, and a gruelling journey flowing out of her as she finally started to relax. Five weeks of good food, good wine and good company in the bosom of her family; what more could one want from life?

At last, her glance rested on my scarred knee, and although I hadn't mentioned my little argument with the stone steps in the Dordogne, it was no surprise to me that her mother had – in great detail and with a summary judgement on the cause, with a "boys will be boys" comment and a raised eyebrow from Alex as she imparted this to me.

Tomorrow we would do the ‘chuck wagon’ run in to Castelnaudary, Alex and Tacey had already done a stock check and were preparing a list of food, whilst Jon and I prepared a separate list for alcohol and soft drinks; he preferred a cordial to be added to the water we were drinking whilst working, whereas I preferred cold water drawn directly from the tap as I found it fresh and palatable enough.

A discussion followed about the various beers and wines available, with careful consideration given to which red wine we would have for the table and which rosé to buy for the girls to drink as an aperitif, or even, if we had fish. The only real decision left was how much wine to buy, reasoning that if we bought too much it wouldn’t be a problem as we could just purchase less next week, so I put down generous numbers on the piece of paper!!!

Jon, Alex and Tacey wouldn’t need me for the visits to the supermarket, butchers and greengrocers, so I decided it would be the opportune moment to have that haircut, because the family could drop me in town, stock up on provisions and collect me on their way back.

12 – A Close Shave in Castelnaudary

After a leisurely breakfast we climbed into the car. Jon was driving and would drop me at the barbers I had previously spotted as we passed through the square.

"Can you manage the French on your own?" they asked me when dropping me off outside the shop "It shouldn't be that difficult, it's only a haircut..." I said as I jumped out of the car giving them a wave as they pulled away.

Inside the barber's shop there were three customers waiting, two of them in uniform, none of them appeared to me to need a haircut, but no doubt there was a regulation length for Legionnaires. The barber had nodded and acknowledged me on arrival and very quickly dealt with the two in uniform.

He was using an electric hair trimmer which could be set to the required length. They duly paid and departed, and the barber moved on to his third client who was dressed like me, as a civilian. After draping this client with the gown, the barber again picked up the trimmer and about three minutes later this customer's head was shaved pretty much the same as the two who had just departed.

I started to panic.

My head in a whirl I realised that it was time to stretch my schoolboy French; how on earth do I say "Just about 2 cm off all over would do nicely please"???

Before I knew it, he had the gown on me, and before I could stutter a word, or gesticulate, the dreaded machine went zoom right up the back of my head!

I stared at the mirror in horror at the picture unfolding in front of me, and realised that it was far too late to do anything about it except to just sit there and let him finish. Well it certainly would be easier to shower I reasoned.

Then it dawned on me, this was the closest barber to the Legionnaires HQ and barracks, he must think that I was just another candidate entrant for the corps!

Having paid merely les "petit sous" (pennies) for this massacre, I stepped outside to wait for the shoppers to return with a little apprehension and a definite chill about my ears. As it had been about an hour since I had been dropped off, I imagined it would not be long before the family turned up to collect me.

Ten minutes later the car came around the top corner of the square heading in my direction. The car slowed as it approached, and I could see the family staring at me from within –collectively shaking their heads, and with a "Drive on! Drive on!" from Alex, Jon sharply accelerated and the car shot straight past me. Very funny I thought, as the car came to a halt some 20m down the road, "I am obviously going to take a lot of stick for this one..."

In the car, I recounted the history of the event which had everybody in stitches along with the inevitable comments like: "When did you get out?", "Never realised what funny ears you have", and "did you know you have an indentation there?" Talk about adding insult to injury, but I knew I had to take it in good humour and so I did, after all it could only improve with time.

On returning to The village, it was all hands to the pump as we did a big unpack and putting away of supplies, Alex took charge as she wanted to make sure that things were where she could find them easily.

Two caravan chest fridges were now plugged in the building in a shaded area to conserve perishables and to chill drinks, with strict orders to all that no drinks to be taken out without restocking.

13 - Judgement Day

Finally the day had arrived, and it was an important one, a make or break one, for us and our little cottage because this was the day we would be going to Bram with Cher (who's French was not bad – thank God!) This would help enormously, irrespective of whether it was good news, or bad.

The appointment was for 11:00 am and I had arranged to pick up Cher at 10:00 and we arrived at her door on the dot. After quick introductions between Alex and Cher (for they had not yet met), and with Don wishing us a quick "Good luck!" we were swiftly on our way.

I speculated whether or not our "to-ing and fro-ing" was being observed, but Cher reassured us that the mayor would not be aware of our meeting at the planning offices, but knowing how internal networks function in the countryside, I was not so sure.

We arrived in Bram with plenty of time to spare and had a bit of a nervous wait in the car before entering the building just before 11. We approached the reception desk and Cher announced who we were, and the name of the official who we were there to see. The receptionist pointed to a seated waiting area and implied that the Monsieur would be with us "Toute suite", which to my surprise, he was!

I found myself shaking hands very formally with a large, thickset gentleman with a big moustache, who then indicated to us to follow him into his office. He had a large desk with his chair on one side and several others for us on the other. He made a very expansive gesture for us to sit, and once we were comfortable he reached for a large file that was on the desk in front of him. Recognising that Cher was the spokesperson, he opened the file whilst Cher confirmed the address of the 'cottage' and handed him the letter we had received from the Mayor.

He duly scrutinised this letter before placing it on the desk in front of him, he then spent several minutes checking through the paperwork in the file, and as is usual in France, there was plenty of it!

With a flourish, and indicating a sort of finality, he closed the file and began to gabble his conclusion to Cher: My heart was in my mouth! Finally she said "Certain sûr?" to which he replied "Weh, définitivement."

Just like that, the meeting ended and he stood up, as we did as well, he shook hands with all of us and we filed out of the office.

As soon as we had all passed through the door, Cher began to explain "The planning consent cannot be withdrawn after approval, irrespective as to who had been mayor when it was granted, and as such it still stands". In other words the mayor was overstepping his authority considerably, and was attempting to pull a fast one hoping that we (the new owners) as English, in our ignorance of the French system, wouldn't realise.

The relief both Alex and I felt was clearly visible and the return drive to the village was much more enjoyable than our journey over to Bram had been. Guided by Cher we went back on the Mirepoix road in order to call at the "yellow sand-seller";

I had already purchased a pack of large polythene garden sacks, and had these, as well as a bucket to use to fill them, in the boot of the car. We soon saw the sign, about a kilometre from Castelnaudary, but that wasn't the only sign we saw, on the gate to the depot was a another sign which when translated said "Closed for August – Annual holiday".

"Ah well you can't win them all".

14 - Flushed with Success

(*And A Reason to Celebrate*)

Back at The village we pulled up at Cher's front door, she got out of the car, and we made promises to invite them all over for a barbeque gathering soon, now that the head cook was here.

We hurried back to the children with the news; which was received with great enthusiasm. Jon stuck two fingers up in the air in the direction towards the Mayor's house and pronounced "Up yours Frenchie!!!" we all laughed, but I added "Now now Jon..."

After lunch, we changed into our working shorts and I said to Jon "Our first task is to get that toilet into working order". I had been thinking that as the internal wall for the toilet was well on its way to completion, and we had the tongue and groove floor boarding of the right depth on site, we could cut boards and place the toilet on them before connecting it to the waste pipe.

The extra bucket I had bought at Bricomarché would provide the water for flushing, with the obligation that every user refill it. "If you cut the board Jon, I will measure the length of the waste connection," I said; it was sticking up by the back wall and sealed with a poly bag, secured in place with a large rubber band.

I quickly whipped these off, and by the stench realised that it must be correctly connected, and because of the smell, immediately replaced the bag and band. Jon returned with the cut planks and immediately I cut the pipe off at the correct height, we then reassembled the toilet, and with the planks in their respective positions, lifted the toilet onto the joint and pressed down.

The toilet connector slid smoothly into place, and Hey Presto! a workable toilet. Jon fetched a bucket of water for me and I gently poured the water into the bowl and thank God this cleared the air of the miasma coming out of the fosse and what's more, there were no leaks!

As Jon started mixing another batch of cement so that we could continue building the bathroom walls, I searched out the good quality toilet seat that Cher had originally bought - primary red would you believe. The girls would even have a perch now for their more delicate backsides! Before long the wall had risen another three blocks which provided a private, lockable area which had plenty of air circulation, as there was still no window or roof!

To celebrate our newly installed toilet, and the great news about the planning permission, we finished earlier than normal and began preparations for the barbecue to which we had invited Don and Cher. We had more than enough beer and wine, but we needed to fill a bucket with very cold water to chill the extra beers that we would use during the evening.

More thought should have gone into the arrangements for seating and tabling, as we only had four camping chairs, Don and Cher would have to supply their own. Our little barbecue would have to cope with the extra demand, but we did have all evening to eat if necessary, and in France meals tend to be long drawn out affairs anyway, so it would be very much in keeping with our environment.

Party Time! A great evening was had by all, and we wondered what with all the sound of laughter and talking reaching the mayor's house, what he would be thinking and we wondered if he already knew the result of our meeting.

15 - The Yellow Sand Search

(And We Dye for a Result!)

Nobody was particular bright or feeling 'workish' the following morning and as the festivities had continued well past midnight it was hardly surprising. After plenty of coffee and a light breakfast we looked at the tasks to be done. Jon would generally tidy up and clean a very dirty barbecue, Tacey would clear what was left of the washing up, whilst Alex and I went into Castelnaudary to try to find an alternative for the yellow sand that we needed to make our window mouldings.

I still couldn't get over the fact that the yellow sand seller would be closed for an entire month, My God how much business would he lose and how typically French? It was devastating; because there was absolutely no way that we could afford to have natural stone, professionally cut by a mason this year, and besides the moulding boxes were all ready to be used.

In the builder's merchant Tangio's I introduced Alex to the girls who shook hands and once again giggled at my attempts at the French language (which I have to admit did contain more than a few English words spoken with a French accent thrown in for good measure).

Alex's French was better than mine and presented the girls with much less of a challenge to understand. Alex explained the situation about our need for yellow sand and the problem we had because the vendor had gone on holiday, to which the girls replied "Weh" and that they were reasonably sure that he did that every year, perhaps their father would be able to suggest something?

They went onto the intercom, and we heard "Papa au Bureau s'il vous plait, Papa au Bureau..." booming across the yard. He shuffled in without much of a delay, and after greeting us both (he was very charming to Alex of course – Italian background I am sure) our problem was discussed.

After a quick fire repartee with his daughters he disappeared into the depths of the warehouse and much to my bemusement reappeared a few moments later brandishing a little bottle in his hand. Seeing my puzzlement he explained that this was a bottle of yellow dye; the bottle had a measuring cap and that we should use one measure per mix of the white cement and sand that they had already delivered to us.

It would not quite be the same as using yellow sand, but the effect achieved would be close enough. He went on to say that the only problem with it was that it was very expensive. Thinking "of course", I asked "Combien?" he flicked his head at one of his daughters and she got out a folder of price lists, and after looking up the product name, wrote a figure down on a piece of paper and handed it over to us. It was over 300 Francs (which at that time would have been around £30.00 give or take), but on the side of the bottle it said that it contained enough for 300 mixes of cement meaning that the cost per mix was only one Franc or 10p, whereas the cost of cut stone would be £200 per window – so it was not hard to see that it was still, for us, good value.

So with five sacks of white cement and our bottle of yellow dye we were back on the road having had another little lesson in French AND French business acumen which was now firmly being embedded into our minds.

Back at The village I told Jon the results of our foray and asked him to barrow the cement from the car into the building and a load of sand to the cement mixer. I was really keen to fill the boxes with a load of our dyed cement so that it could set over the weekend; we would start with the bathroom window which would be fitted with three and a half moulded blocks on each side.

The mixing went well, we used slightly more white cement than I would normally use for pointing, and after brushing the insides of the moulds with diesel fuel, to prevent sticking, and fixing the battens and dividers correctly, we were soon pouring the mixture in. Using another two battens as tools we tamped down the mixture into the moulds to get rid of any air holes or bubbles, and then left them to set. "Exciting" said Jon;

we were both looking forward to the following week when this work would be exposed to show us how yellow they would actually appear.

We then made a normal mix of cement and continued with the bathroom wall by laying another row which was now eight blocks high. This was bringing us nearly to the completion of the wall, and as we felt now that the Maire's objection had been removed, we returned to working on the cemetery wall.

There was absolutely no doubt in my mind that by now, the mayor would be fully aware of the ruling concerning the planning permission.

16 - A Visit to the Lake

The pillar at the end of the cemetery wall had already been erected and was solid, so a builder's line was taken from it to the front of the cottage, to mark the height and extent of building needed on that side. It would raise that piece of cemetery wall by approximately two feet when completed and knit into the cottage wall.

We had plenty of stone already sorted at the moment, removed from what would be the openings of the door and window to the courtyard, so the work progressed well.

It was very hot and Jon and I had been working without shirts at every opportunity and had already started to tan, while Tacey a real sun lover would also return to England the envy of all her friends. On Sunday we would go to the lake, just a few miles away, take a picnic and have a swim.

Everyone was quite excited at the prospect; it would make a fantastic break from the monotony that Tacey was enduring although she was much happier now she had her mother about the place. So another productive day drew to an end, and after the excruciating heat, how good the shower was. We were really getting the hang of it and with careful timing; everyone was receiving a fair share of warm water.

Sunday was to be our day of rest, and the visit to the lake. There was a rug in the car but a couple of chairs would be useful, and the folding table could go in the boot. "Don't forget your costumes and towels" Alex said.

Before setting off Jon and I could not resist taking a quick look at the moulds resting quietly against the cool wall of the interior of the cottage, out of the way so as not to be damaged by other activities.

I gave them a closer examination and they seemed to be hardening well, but the most satisfying factor was the colour. Not as bright as cut stone but much yellower than the natural stone we were using and would be a great contrast when finished.

The lake was in fact a reservoir of approximately half a mile across and there were several people already out and enjoying it. There were no swimming restrictions on this near side, which was served by a dusty, gravelled car park, and we were soon unpacked and installed on a grassy bank that sloped towards the lake. Jon, Tacey and I had decided on a quick dip before lunch as the temperature was already climbing.

Before we left the caravan the thermometer had already reached 27°C, and now although there was a slight breeze coming across the water it was going to get really hot. Jon and I were soon changed and tiptoeing into beautiful, clear cool water, but we soon discovered the downside. There was about four inches of soft mud underfoot, which didn't feel at all pleasant. Never mind, we hurried into deeper water and were soon swimming, splashing and laughing. Tacey did not like the mud at all but was soon out of it and getting a good cooling and enjoying a swim.

Afterwards, lying on a rug to dry, and gazing up into a cloudless, blue sky, I spotted a large number of Condors that had drifted up towards us from Spain. At an enormous height, they were just dots and they were not flying, but drifting on the air currents.

A clattering of plates brought me back from my reverie, and I pointed out to the others what I had seen. It took them a moment to adjust their eyesight to the distance and were amazed at the flying height and we speculated how thin the air might be up there. Jon thought that as they didn't need to expend any energy as they drifted, they perhaps wouldn't need much oxygen.

After our picnic we read and lazed in the sun, and now a breeze was rising over the water and the girls were putting on sun cream protection. Jon, cheeky toad, suggested I put some on my ears, leading to laughter. But Alex said that some cream on the nape of my neck might be a precaution after the haircut, as it was already a bit pink, and that sunstroke would be very unpleasant. Some sense prevailing after the joke.

We had been watching a wind surfer way on the other side of the lake and now with the breeze getting up; he was having a great time and was slowly tacking towards us. As he neared we noticed something else, he had no clothes on. We stared and Jon asked "what do you think he is steering with?" He soon worked his way back to the far bank, where, I imagine there was no swimming, which had afforded him the privacy for his jaunt.

What a lovely, quiet, restful Sunday, and as we made our way slowly back to The village we decided that the lake had been a grand discovery, and even to slip over for a dip after work would be feasible and afford great relief from the heat yet to come.

17 - Pillars and Pilloried

We were now at the beginning of another week, and so back to our moulds. We were both anxious to reveal the result of our first setting, so armed with a screwdriver, a lump hammer and a bolster (a wide stone chisel) we carefully turned them over.

I then tapped the bottoms, not too hard for fear of cracking them and... Nothing happened; they seemed as well wedged in as before. We lifted the box slightly and tapped again with the hammer, we saw the end of the block move, and so then we "trigged" the other end up and repeated the procedure and the two blocks, one at each end, seemed free, but the middle section was still clinging to the box.

"OK" I said, we still needed maximum care, we took off one side, which came away quite easily, then having removed the batten, we tapped the other side. I sensed movement and we carefully rolled the whole thing over and out they came, one after the other, a flake or two came off the edges, but really, really fascinating and pleasing.

I ran my thumbnail down one and yes, still very green, (not hard and dry) but fit to handle. We carefully set them aside and repeated the process with the other box, and soon, we had six blocks.

Fantastic, clean the boxes with a stiff brush and then measure what was needed to finish the sides to the top of the window. We needed two short pieces and the spare piece would give us the first block of one side of the doorway.

From the other box we removed the spacers completely, as this was to be the lintel of the window, having lengths of steel in the middle for strength to support the roof. Jon would have to mix enough cement for building the pillars and the lintel, so he made up two mixes to give us sufficient for both operations.

Having already done the first two moulds, no time was lost with the next two; we would probably be able to place the lintel at the end of the week. These are the moments when the building suddenly changes and you get the transformation from ruin to potential house.

The area at the bottom of the window, which would be the sill, was carefully cleaned and prepared for the base, which had to be level, and after checking twice, the first pillar was put into place.

We had cut battens at exactly the width of the window, but the vertical had to be measured and marked. Each block would be some forty kilograms in weight at least, which would require much care and accuracy, and muscle power to put into position, For this effort I was wearing my customary back support.

The first two blocks were now in place and if we completed the wall to them they would be well supported on that one side, and when the window was placed it would be supported from both sides. There only remained to drill holes through the frame and to screw it to the pillars, and HEY we have a secure and stone framed window.

A good lunch, and my usual nap after eating and we would continue, or so I thought. Alex tapped on the door to wake me, and I could hear Jon talking to someone in French. I got up and put on my working shorts and stepped out. Alex, pointing, said “we have a visitor”.

Standing in *our* garden was a young Gendarme, fully uniformed, with the customary gun on belt, obviously on an official visit. In later years we came to realise that sense of humour they have not, and after we had greeted him with a smile, which was not reciprocated, he asked who we were, and could we show him our passports?

Bien sur, was our polite response. Alex went into the caravan and returned with the passports for the whole family which he studied intently, looking at each picture and indentifying each of us as he gave them close scrutiny.

Finally, he came to Alex, and giving her a stern look he said in his strong Southern accent “Liverpool? Ou est Liverpool?” Before we could stop him, our son blurted “you know, where the hooligans come from” referring to a recent football disturbance.”Ooligans “ he said “ooligans?”, and Alex had to step in quickly to diffuse the situation whilst giving Jon a meaningful glare. When asked what we were doing here, and now being sure he was not daft, we explained that we were renovating OUR property.

After this he muttered something, something “Finis “and departed. For about half an hour after he left we discussed the situation and decided that this was the result of an action by a spoilt and annoyed Mayor who had been outflanked, and was just trying to make us feel uncomfortable.

We had no idea if he had other plans to make our situation difficult. “What to do about it?” Alex asked, I said I would sleep on it, but that it would not halt us in what we had planned for the summer.

The next day we continued with our mornings work and by the evening great progress had been made on the bathroom window and door. As soon as the lintel had cured (dried solid) we would be moving forward. We needed to keep the boxes full as fast as we could, and continue with casting for all the windows for the cottage.

Our system was followed to the letter. We just let the casting control our progress. By now we had run out of the stone gleaned from the window and door. We would now take out the stone for the next cottage window, and that would serve two purposes: give us the material for the wall work and prepare the next window for the lintels.

18 - A Visit to the Mairie

The following morning, I said I was going to see the Mayor, and asked Alex to come with me. "What's the objective" she asked, and I answered "Charm Offensive".

We would introduce ourselves to him formally, and then explain to him what we had planned for the cottage, and smile a lot. Just up Alex' street. "Good", she said "there are more ways to kill a cat, and he won't be expecting this sort of approach. Hopefully it will take the wind out of his sails".

So we dressed up in our going out to eat garb, casual smart, walked across the square and knocked at his door which was at the side of his house and out of sight from our cottage.

After a few minutes a short, dark woman opened the door and we asked if we could speak to Mr Fosse the mayor. She left us standing there and returned into the depths of the house. "First ice broken" I said to Alex.

We heard footsteps, and here was the mayor, tall, dark and clean shaven. He obviously recognised me, and as I introduced Alex, and tried to explain that she was a schoolteacher, which I hoped might impress him, and Alex explained that is why she had followed us down to Perpignan by coach from London as her school term had finished after the family's departure.

He showed some sympathy for her lengthy journey. He's almost human I thought. We would like to outline to him what we had in mind for the cottage, I explained. He said 'oui' and we followed him into his office in the house. I introduced the plan and explained that the renovation would take a while, and be achieved over several holidays, as we both had work and other obligations back in England.

This was not that easy in our broken French, but we realised this was an educated man and he was being patient.

We produced the plan and pointed out the areas of activity for this summer and suggested that if he would care to call round at any time we would be happy to see him. To which he agreed. Result! We both observed on our way back across the square.

He did come over after a few days, and leant over from the churchyard side, standing on some other families tomb, I might add, and said that as I had such a great reputation as a renovator, (who is on the charm offensive now?) he was sure I would be able to keep all guttering well back on the wall, and clear of the graveyard. I nodded sagely, and said that I would do my best.

Alex enquired later as to how I would approach that request from Fosse, and I answered. That as from the top end of the little cottage to the end of the extension was quite some distance, and I'd not measured it or made an exact calculation, but assuming the length of the cottage was six metres, and the extension ten metres, a narrow gutter would not be sufficient to carry the normal volume of water, let alone the torrents that would fall in a thunder storm as we had witnessed last week.

This waste water would then be returned to our own property to a soakaway near the bottom corner of the garden by the fig tree. Bearing in mind the size of the guttering that I would need to use, and that I was not prepared to compromise the building, as he was suggesting, I would keep it as close to the wall as possible.

We must just hope that with the situation having been diffused, that his attitude would soften as the summer passed. We would now put all of that behind us, and if we saw him or any of his family, we would greet them with a smile; we would carry on with our pretence of "bonhomie" with the charm offensive continuing throughout the summer.

There was a small vegetable patch below us, with the access to it down a track at the side of our garden wall. This, we understood, belonged to the mother of the maire and indeed, this old lady had appeared, perhaps twice a week to gather, and guard what little she had planted that year.

Dressed all in black, as is the widows uniform throughout rural France, she looked like an old black crow flapping about down there. She would definitely be included in the charm offensive, as she was no doubt, the eyes and ears of the maire as to what was going on this side of the square.

The system of keeping the moulds full, and keeping moving forward with each batch was serving Jon and I perfectly. Our progress was controlled by this process and gave momentum to the build.

It was now time to start sorting the timber for the roof. We had on site a prepared pillar of hardwood which would be sited vertically in the middle of the front of the extension. It would support one end of a large beam which would reach to the corner of the new bathroom wall.

The width of this room towards the front, looking out onto the garden, increased and so needed this extra support for the roof. The idea was that the roof would include the ceiling, which when painted and finished, would resemble a sandwich.

Cross timbers which were grooved and stained, had been prepared to receive the ceiling boards which were secured at forty centimetres apart. The insulation was rolled out on top of these boards, with another layer of boarding on top, then the felt secured by battens, finishing with the tiles! Simple, we have a finished roof sandwich!

19 - Monsegur

(A Massacre on a Mountain)

Another Sunday, another outing, this time to find Monsegur, a Cathar castle. It was a beautiful, bright and promising morning for our day out, and over breakfast, maps were out to prepare a route up the slopes of the Pyrenees.

Luncheon picnic prepared, coffee flasks filled, and everyone excited at the prospect of breaking our work routine. Alex had done quite a bit of research about the Cathar religious movement that had so dominated the life in this area centuries ago, and many fascinating details about them and their beliefs had been discussed. We would try to create a circular route to take in some other points of interest on the way. We left the village heading towards Mirepoix, and the distant views of the mountains.

As we meandered through these dusty side roads we spotted the occasional flocks of sheep, and noticed the distinct pattern of their grazing behaviour. Always, but always, grazing in a circle with heads towards the centre, "so why", asked Tacey "do they have this extraordinary habit? "Well", I explained with all my farming and sheep expertise coming to the fore!! "Flies," I said, "there are two very bothersome species of fly that arrive with this heat: one searching for moisture from their eyes and mouths, and the other searching for blood by biting the interior of their nostrils.

They endeavour to protect each other by grazing in this clever formation, with the flies finding it more difficult to feed off them as they cover each other." Jon said, "Just like an army forming a block defence." "A little more like self preservation" I remarked.

The hills appeared a little closer now, and the higher ranges seemed much clearer and some snow was still evident on the upper reaches. The countryside was slowly changing as we climbed, leaving the arable areas far behind, and with more evidence of stock farms, with smaller flocks of sheep and stocky beef animals.

Many more water courses of clear moving water were now descending from the slopes above, which Jon and I were eying with enthusiasm, as we remembered our own fishing experiences in fast flowing, gin clear brooks of the Westcountry, that, with some luck, gave us trout of an exceptional flavour.

It was approaching coffee time, and for some while we had been seeing brown tourist signs for Fontetorbes ahead. A good place to stop, as our research team had it flagged as a "must see", it was a 'Karst Spring' - a river rising from deep underground through a cave that released huge volumes of water recurring very regularly every 40 minutes. We then discussed, until we arrived there, the siphonage system that nature must have provided for this phenomenon to occur.

There were many people already there and waiting when we arrived and we were advised that the surge would occur in another ten minutes, so we had time to walk into the cave along a raised pathway that had a handrail for safety, and waited.

Quite weird, no sound, no warning, but suddenly the waters started to rise and nearly everybody ran out. Those who chose to wait would be quite safe until the level of the waters dropped again, albeit with wet feet. It was their choice. It was an extraordinary experience, and we stayed to see it happen for a second time before continuing on our way to the Cathar castle of Monsegur.

A short time later we had our first view of the castle, starkly outlined on what seemed to be the top of a mountain a short time later, and could not believe that anyone in their right mind would choose to build all the way up there.

It was huge and foreboding and thoughts of the persecutions that this religious sect had suffered were vivid in our imaginations. We found it hard to understand why they were feared or loathed so much as we had read that the leaders (or Perfects) did not believe in procreation, and we thought that if the pope at the time had just waited they would have eventually died out! Although we understood that the Cathars at Monsegur had all been incinerated in the castle, our later research indicated that they had, in fact, been slaughtered and their bodies burnt at the foot of the mountain.

Jon had been very interested in the speculation over the centuries, about their wealth and The Holy Grail, which was said to have somehow been spirited away. These stories had been lent some credence by the interest shown by Himmler and his researchers in the 1930's.

I sensed that we would be treated to another burst of the Monty Python sketch "and whose castle is this?" (from Jon) in a terrible French accent from him and his sister before long. Up, up, up we wound our way with our objective coming ever closer and it was even more imposing the nearer we got, and eventually we arrived at the car park where assorted coaches and cars were already lined up.

For us, lunch first and then "who's for the climb?" as the rest of the way was on foot. Once more it would be trying for my back, but with the aid of the support belt, I could probably manage and I was keen not to miss the complete experience of this strangely compelling place. I could, of course, always turn back if the going got too hard.

We packed away our picnic; made sure we had sensible footwear, and made our way to the start of the path. More track than path, and all care must be taken as a tumble up near the top would not be too clever. There seemed to be groups of "deciders" at the foot of the path who were either not confident, or of a certain age group who were erring on the side of caution, but I was not one of them.

Off we set, and we were soon part of the way up, taking a rest from time to time, to admire the views of the distant areas and mountains, as we climbed higher.

I was now more aware of the hawks swooping and wheeling at this height, it was obviously part of their hunting and resting area with rocky outcrops, scrub and gorse interspersed with small clearings. Ideal habitat for small rodents, rabbits, hares and smaller ground nesting birds, apart from providing areas where the constant stream of visitors could stop to catch breath and admire the stunning views.

It really was quite a challenging climb which made us wonder all the more about the numbers of workers that must have taken part in its construction. Eventually we arrived in its huge keep and walking the path around the wall admired the views which were absolutely spectacular.

Miles and miles of countryside stretching all the way back the way we had come, and on the other side the range of higher and higher peaks of the Pyrenees. The very highest gleaming white with existing snow and away to the other side, Spain.

We sat for some while contemplating all this with wonder that a religious sect could isolate itself in this way and indeed that the Catholic hierarchy felt that the threat from them made it necessary for such determined pursuit and annihilation.

Our return home by another route was through gorges beside rushing rivers bordered by lush foliage, and it needed extra careful driving as the road often returned to single carriageway when overhanging rock made it necessary. On one occasion two French drivers had arrived nose to nose at one such section and sat there hooting and gesticulating at each other, neither wanting to give way.

A mediator was delegated from among the waiting drivers, who were now queued up behind on both sides, and supported by about twenty more, managed to sort things out. Our family were in stitches watching their hand, arm and shoulder actions. You really could not have been anywhere else but in France!

The countryside was becoming much more familiar and we realised we were now looking over the valley of the Entre Deux Mers and soon we were trundling back into the square.

20 - Groovy Man...

So now we come to the saga of the dreaded router. Don had a router and had given some of his timbers a decorative ceiling edge finish. He had offered to lend it to us if we wanted it. My thought was to use it to cut the slot to receive the ceiling boarding.

So a quick visit to Don who wasn't using it and with the cutter bit already fitted, he handed it over. We then began sorting out the timbers we were going to need for the roof. One or two of them, in their drying out process had assumed a slight banana shape, and we put these aside, not to discard, but if one was put in now and again amongst the straight ones, it should not take too much effort to force it into place by cramping it to the beams that were already secured.

We had our workbench and two trestles to secure the timbers to whilst working on them. The grooves each side with the timbers thus anchored would be easy to cut, and a hole at each end for the eventual nailing would complete the preparation.

First of all, of course, the pillar and beam had to be in place, and we carried them into what now had become the work place and not yet the dining room. So, prepare a joint at the top of the centre prop to receive the end of the beam, and then placing a taut builder's line across the front, and pulling it really tight to establish the height. Cut the beam to exact length, drill a hole in the base of the prop dead centre, and drive a steel bar in, leaving some 5 centimetres protruding. Drilling a hole in the floor to receive the steel bar would hold it in a secure position, so then we have only to check that it was vertical to be in its final resting place.

So, one, two, three and heave, now we had it upright; Jon straining and holding it steady, and balancing it on its point, was not the easiest job. I put my arms around it and with Jon in that same position we heaved together and moved it the few inches to the receiving hole. With a satisfying clunk it slid into place: what a bit of luck, I had imagined much more effort would be needed before we hit the actual spot.

We then secured it with a couple of battens and stood back to admire the result. Jon laughing said, "That's as good an erection as anyone would see" and I laughed, ah boys will be boys I thought.

Now we had to fix the pillar permanently by securing the beam between it and the new wall of the bathroom. One end at a time, and the wall end first, as that was stable, which was very soon achieved with the assistance of our new steps, then with the scaffold at the other end, slowly we placed it on the top of the pillar. Fine, the really heavy part was over, so now cutting grooves, planing corners, cutting ceiling boards, staining and treating.

Treating timber against death watch beetle and hornbeetle is very important out there. They are rampant in these temperatures and are ever present in the forests around and about. So we would start with the timbers at both ends, from the new wall to the front. Having secured the two big timbers we must now secure the vertical, it must not be able to move.

This was now like a production line, the first timbers would be cut and prepared and fixed at once, so the selection had to be absolutely straight for the first two or three rows. We needed a really true and square frame in order to fix the slightly curved timbers.

All was going well and several timbers had been prepared, but the router was not dealing with the groove too well and it seemed that it needed a new blade as the cutter kept filling and blocking progress. So after preparing six timbers, we decided that after treating and staining them, we would make a quick visit to Brico for new blade/blades before we continued.

Before that though, I wanted to prepare one of the banana shaped timbers to sandwich between the straight ones. We cut it to length and marked the position of the groove and secured it to the bench and started to groove it on one side. Very slow, we did need a new blade, but finally we finished that side, unclamping and turning it over.

Calamity! The bend made it spin suddenly and fall, knocking the router off the bench as it went. The machine hit the concrete floor with a sickening thud, Jon and I looked at each other in horror and I bent to pick it up. A piece of the thick plastic bottom that helped to guide the blade had broken off. It would have to be replaced before returning to Don. 'Never a borrower or a lender be' was the old maxim and it was never truer than at this minute!

Well there was no point delaying the awkward moment. I had to own up to Don immediately so I carried it as one would a dead pet, I felt sick. I reluctantly knocked on the door, and Cher opened it, greeted me, and looked at what I had in my arms and said gravely "I'll fetch Don" He arrived and looking sadly at the disaster that I presented to him, agreed that the lower part of the machine did appear to be screwed on, but would have to be renewed. Don believed that there was a small machine engineer who dealt with Black and Decker, at Toulouse, and this machine was one of their professional range.

We sat at his table while he searched the Yellow Pages France through the Toulouse index. After a while he grunted "Ah" and wrote the name and address and telephone number of their unit, which was on the outskirts of the city. Could he ring them and check that they could help, and we would take it over immediately. Cher, with her excellent French was soon talking to their office, and after having provided the serial number of the machine, they confirmed that it could be repaired and/or the part replaced, if necessary.

So armed with the address and phone number we went back to the caravan to discuss schedules. It being lunchtime we decided to eat, clean up a bit and depart after we had eaten.

Jon was always keen to drive, and I studied a map of Toulouse, which was difficult to read, to find where this light industrial area was. It would take at least the better part of the afternoon to get this sorted: we had no idea whether it could be fixed right away, or in fact it would have to be left to wait for a new part. At least an hour and a quarter to Toulouse, find the estate sort out answers and return. Sad, what a waste of productive time but we had no option, so off we went.

Good progress was made to the outskirts of town but we experienced quite some difficulty finding the estate, but eventually, and taking care to remember the road for our return, we found it.

There were, maybe forty different companies on this industrial site. We made a tour and found it towards the end of our circuit.

We gathered up the stricken machine and entered. At the desk we were greeted by an elderly fellow with a moustache, who on seeing the damaged router said that he had been expecting us. He examined it carefully and explained that they would enquire from Black and Decker about a new part, but in the possible event of there being nothing available for this older model, they would attempt to pin and glue. Could we ring again in a week and they would give us the answer?

On our return, I said to Jon that we could not afford to wait, that it would lose us more valuable time and that I thought that perhaps a visit to Brico on the way back would be sensible. All in all we made good time on the return journey, and were in the store soon after five o'clock. We went straight to the electrical department and there they had a Bosch router, a handy man tool, not their professional line. Still, it looked the business, and had been discounted to about £60. Plenty of cutting bits to fit it were included, and those in the Bricolage line were less than half the price of Bosch's own, so we bought two of these as spares. Well pleased with our purchases, and happy that the work would not be further interrupted we drove on back to The village.

Immediately after breakfast the next morning, Jon started treating and staining the first timbers, and I would complete the grooves with the new machine on the piece of wood that had caused all the heartache. No, the same thing didn't happen again; all went well for about half a metre and then it blocked. I cleared the blade, did another small piece and the same thing happened again, only sooner this time.

This start and stutter continued for about an hour, and finally I said to Jon that I could only think that this motor hadn't sufficient power for the operation. Jon wondered if it was a faulty blade and said "Don't forget that Dons machine was struggling to keep cutting the groove. So, try a new blade", which was circular and had about six cutting edges, set at an angle to reject the shavings, and it felt really sharp. So I tried again with exactly the same result. It didn't seem to matter how slowly one proceeded, after a few centimetres it would block once more.

I looked at the pile that needed to be grooved in despair; it would take hours and hours to put two grooves in each. Jon said he would like to try, which he did, but with same useless result.

"What do we do now dad" he said, "Well" I said "first of all I'm going to clean the dust off this piece of shit, box it up and return it" Do they do that in France he wondered "I don't know but we are going to try" was my reply "and in the meantime I'm going to attempt an experiment".

Setting the electric saw to half an inch of depth, mark for two cuts one centimetre apart and take the waste out with a sharp narrow chisel and mallet. He helped me mark out the next timber, and I carefully cut the two grooves. Then I started tapping and splitting out the groove, and apart from the occasional knot that had to be carefully cut and negotiated, it worked a treat, and one timber was finished in no time. "Well I'd wish I'd tried this in the first place and had never heard of a bloody router" I said. Using this method we made speedy progress, and that afternoon would see the timbers complete. Then stain and treat and leave to dry.

21- Dave and Girls Arrive

(And a Roof Goes On)

After lunch that day as we continued the staining, we heard a vehicle arriving in the square. Doors slamming and I looked out of the bathroom window to see a man coming around the corner of the old forge.

It was a long time friend called Dave, followed by his wife Trish and their three little girls. On seeing me he grinned, and flicked his ears in compliment to my military style haircut.

At this point, I should explain that he had been a training sergeant in the marines: a career soldier who had served tours in Northern Ireland, been present at other hot spots during his service, including the Falklands, retiring shortly afterwards. You could say we were both marked by our careers to date, with me resembling a broken down nag fit for the

Knackers yard, but very much by my own hand, and his by serving the British government and the misfortunes of war.

I had spoken to him in the spring about our summer plan, and he said "We are going over to France this summer with the caravan, we may call in!", but it had been a casual, throwaway remark and I had thought no more about it. He now asked if we could use an extra hand for a week, and thinking of the roof we were preparing, I naturally jumped at his offer. So, rearrange the garden to accommodate two caravans, and car parking.

We could manhandle them both facing each other, still leaving plenty of room behind his for the shower, and making a shared dining area between the two awnings. The two families knew each other very well, and Trish, Alex and Tacey were soon chattering away, sharing recent news while the three little girls explored the site. They all trooped into the roofless extension and spotting the toilet they took advantage of the opportunity.

Dave thought this was magical and rushing for his camera, put a brolly in the hand of his middle daughter who was enthroned at the time. A family photograph to remind us of that moment. Dave soon picked up on our forward plan for the roof and the necessity for a speedy schedule. Before tiling, the insulation had to be put between the rafters, then felt, batten and tile. Sounds easy when said quickly, but one could not get it out of sequence as it was one layer after another.

Alex and Trish had agreed that because of the restrictions that went with catering from a caravan and the limited sizes of our barbeques, each family would cook for themselves but would have their aperos, dinner and coffees together. This way there would be no extra stress on either cook. Trish really was set up for outdoor living in the grand manner, and that first night set up her picnic table complete with a tablecloth and also a candelabra!

The arrival of friends, and another set of willing hands would provide a boost and make a huge difference to our progress.

Over supper later that night, I related the sad story of the router to Dave, and explained that I was intending to return it on our next shopping trip and he observed “Well you will have to do this in French, apart from their difference in consumer rules. Good luck mate”.

The weather was absolutely brilliant, but now the heat was starting to affect Alex, never too comfortable with very high temperatures. We needed the roof to give a bit more protection from the sun. Could we get it on in a two day operation? “Well” said Alex “When you are ready for the tiles we will form a human chain, won’t we guys?” Three little girls and three bigger ones all nodded. Great idea and many hands would certainly help. “But you must take care with the sharp edges on the clay tiles” I warned.

So the three of us put on the load bearing beams, with ceiling in place, cramped and nailed any banana timbers, and soon we were ready for the insulation.

A series of wide planks were temporarily pinned in place as a platform for us to work off. We didn’t want anyone to fall through the ceiling at this stage. The rolls of insulation went on quickly: they were the right width for the job and unwound across the roof like a dream. We now had to felt and batten, so starting at the lower edge in order to give an overlap, we were soon advancing up the roof in eighty centimetres widths, each overlapping as we went. Once the felt and batten operation was complete we could relax a little as it was now dry underneath, and the felt would give plenty of protection on a wet day or from a thunderstorm.

Everybody was now gathered below looking at the transformation from a big ‘open to the sky’ area, to a large room. The roof in place made the room look really huge. The perspective had totally changed. It was quite remarkable, now the girls would have a covered, insulated area to retreat to if necessary, and after we had tiled the roof tomorrow we could then begin to lay a lovely wooden floor. What excitement!

The next day showed early signs of being hot again, with the sun gaining strength as it crept up over the cottage wall and eventually to the roof. An early start for all I think. I can't wait to see the effect that the melange of orange and yellow pantiles will produce. A cord line already in place to give a straight beginning and move the line up as each course demanded.

The little ones passing the tiles to the bigger ones, Trish part way up the ladder passing to Dave and on to Jon before I placed it. What a system, and the progress we were making, was incredibly fast, considering the size of the roof. Coffee time, and Alex broke off, but the work continued with tiles arriving like clockwork. In a few minutes, a yell from the garden "coffee ready" and we took a break. I could not believe it, as at least half the roof was now in place. Many hands did indeed make light work. Brilliant effort, at this rate we could have them all up there by lunch time.

22 - A Cunning Cornish Plan

A quieter and lazier afternoon after the rush of the morning, then after a break a run to Castelnaudary for more provisions would be needed. Trish and Dave needed to stock up as well, and I needed to face up to Mr Bricolage with the dreaded router. So in the middle of the afternoon we set off, Tacey decided not to come and would gladly look after any, or all of Trish's girls. Jon and I together would take on Mr Brico and decided to make our call on the way.

As it turned out, the afternoon being so hot we all entered the store to get out of the heat in preference to waiting in the car. An assistant arrived, no doubt thinking Ah! the English, "Big Spenders!" and seemed rather taken aback when we handed him the box explaining that we wished to return the router as it was not fit for purpose. At this stage it almost seemed as if we were playing pass the parcel, because he then thrust it back at us. We asked to see the manager, the Chef.

These outlets, as with many stores in France seemed to be franchises and normally the boss would be on the premises, possibly in the office. Well after a short delay he arrived, or rather, waddled, and approached us with, I felt, some reluctance, and asked what the problem was.

We explained that it would not perform the task we expected of it, and would like to return it. We passed him the parcel, which he opened, and took out the machine, and exclaimed "but you have used it" and my reply "well how do you think I knew it is not powerful enough for the work?"

Well, Mr Fatz as we now called him, with his apparent fear of taking something back that had already been paid for, was visibly breaking out in a sweat, and along with this sad affliction, a waft of B O wafted our way. We both blanched, and to me it seemed a sign of weakness, and I repeated my request, as I was sure that a purchaser had this right, but he refused, and handed me the parcel with finality and pronounced "Ce n'est pas possible Monsieur".

Feeling really deflated I found Alex who had been perusing round the store, returned to the car, and set off for the shopping. We explained what had happened between us, and he, who will forever now be referred to as Mr Fatz, along with the aroma issues, and she observed “So no consumer rights at all here in France then.”

We did a big shop and were returning along the route that passed by Brico once more.”Pull in Jon,” I said “I’m going in to have another go at Mr Fatz” “you are joking” from Alex and a “What’s the angle Dad?” from Jon.

Well as we had been leaving the store earlier I had seen a big insulated water heater, something we would be needing very soon for the bathroom and kitchen, and as it was rather more expensive than the router had been, I said “I think I will try a little cunning Cornish barter” and picked up the offending boxed machine. Mr Fatz was out and about in the store, and when he spotted us entering again, he tried to scarper, (in his condition?), back to his office, but we had him cornered.

Naturally he began to sweat and smell, but I was determined not to be deflected from my objective. “We intend to spend much more money in your store, starting with that heater over there, near the front”.

“Weh” he said suspiciously, he realised of course there was more to come. “But only if you credit us with the returned router”. So we had a big fat and smelly Frenchman cornered, and deciding between making a profit and his damaged pride. He looked us over and said “you will take the heater now?” “Weh” was my reply. Profit had won, and we could retreat with honour and with reputation intact, with a large water heater strapped onto the roof. Dave and family were hugely amused to hear the Mr Fatz story that evening and we raised a glass to him.

23 - Floored by the Result

So now we had a roof over the extension giving protection from wet and heat, also a comfortable working/resting/eating area inside. A line would be drawn across the front central pillar, which would mark the extent of the living area. We would lay the wooden floor from that line to the doorway of the old cottage.

The timbers supporting the cottage bedrooms would be prepared, and inserted into the walls to support the floor upstairs. I needed to improvise a staircase to enable us to work safely on the upper level, and also to build the windows of the cottage.

We decided that Dave would fill the moulds, and start removing the stonework for windows, whilst Jon would cut and pass floorboards to me as required. Dave said that he always felt happier with a shovel in his hands, so that was fine. After first filling the boxes he would continue with the downstairs window in what would be the sitting room, which eventually would have a chimney and wood burner.

We measured and marked out the size of the window which looked out onto the courtyard. The spoil could be taken out that way and the good stone stacked behind him. We worked well as a team, and the banter and laughter was hugely infectious.

The memory of this time and of the happiness and satisfaction with the project has remained with me in all the years that have followed.

The floor board laying advanced quickly, and disguised nailing through the tongue to the timbers set in the concrete, gave a superb finish. Our progress was being admired by all as we worked our way back through the room. Each board was tightened back to the previous one to produce a perfect surface.

The first section back to the kitchen wall and to the foot of the steps up to the bathroom would be completed, we hoped, by the end of the day. Dave had filled the boxes with the yellow mix and was now attacking the wall where the window was to be.

Over supper that evening we decided that we had now reached a reasonable stopping point for the time being, as the following weekend was to be the village fete, and as is the normal tradition of the children, (and in this village mainly children of local farmers), had already been around collecting donations to help towards the cost of bunting, music etc.

Cher told us it was a very popular local event, and that people came from miles around to enjoy it. At least three lambs would be barbequed. There would be a large boules/petanque competition, which we found was taken very seriously indeed, and with music and dancing that went on through the night.

The celebration started on the Friday night and continued for the whole of the weekend, and ended late on Sunday. Our decision was to embrace it, as we doubted anyway, that we would achieve much for those three days at least. The tickets for the meal were already being sold, and Cher said that she would reserve ours for us. Our reservations were made, half price for the little ones.

We were all looking forward to it and were amused to see tractors with forklifts and trailers being used to assist the organisers hang their decorations around the village square. We were happy to see waves and smiles coming our way from these workers, which was encouraging after our initial reception only a couple of weeks ago.

We reckoned we had a few hours left in which to work, before the workers, tractors and ladders were removed, and people started to arrive for the beginning of the festivities. In spite of their activities, our work was attracting attention as well. They didn't turn up and stand and stare, but it seemed obvious that very little was being missed because of the looks coming in our direction, discussions and nodding of heads. At this time, in this area, at least, Englishmen renovating old buildings were a rarity. We were in no doubt that after our departure at the end of August there would be closer inspections.

By late in the afternoon we would certainly finish the flooring through the hallway. We would leave the section of the doorway of the bathroom ready to knit in tomorrow.

Dave was having a wonderful time taking out the lounge window opening, and a good pile of stones was now stacked, and ready to use for the walls upstairs. Now for the temporary staircase to the second storey: It would need to be sturdy enough to take our weight, and that of the heavy materials that we would be carrying up them, and above all safe, but not permanent so that any damage on the treads would not matter.

We had an oversupply of timber bought for the flooring and the roof, so I could utilise some of it for this staircase. The opening to receive it was already established by the position of the floor timbers upstairs, and so I would put two long timbers on edge to form the sides, and then mark them with the angle top and bottom, remove them and cut the marked waste off. Place one in position, and Wow it would be the Dogs Bollocks!

Now came the more difficult part, measuring precisely the position for the steps; they were to be approximately eighteen centimetres apart, top to bottom. We used the first long timber as a template, remembering that the grooves must face each other exactly, and then repeating the operation for the remainder. I would give Jon the measurements for the width of the steps and he (using a very clever mathematic formula) would calculate and cut the number required, whilst I hacked out the grooves to receive them. So that by the time we broke off for the fete weekend, most of the work I had scheduled would be complete. We would just need a couple of sheets of hard board to work off on the second floor in the coming week. Good progress.

24 - The Fete

(Of Everyone!)

We broke off early on that Friday, and the shower schedule had to be very carefully worked out. Dave, roughy, toughy marine that he was, said he would grab a big bowl of water and retire to the bathroom. All the girls, who had had their showers a little earlier, seemed to be on the hunt for mirrors. What excitement!

We were all going to gather for drinks, and have the two barbeques working in tandem. There were people arriving in the square, some to work on the bar, and at others to man small amusement stands that had been set up. A large farm trailer had been parked at an angle by the old forge. It had a big tarpaulin cover over the top of a frame, and very soon a live band arrived to get their acoustic equipment set up, accessing mains electricity etc.

Several children were now turning up, the girls in party dresses, and dashing around like spring lambs, and of course occasionally falling over. Their reaction to Les Anglais was quite different to that of the adults. They would come up quite close, stand and stare at us with their dark, dark eyes. When we did the same and caught their eyes, the boys darted off laughing, while the girls did a sort of swinging motion with their skirts, and then flounced away.

The music was warming up and people were now gathering, many coming together in family groups, we suspected not having seen each other for some time. The bar was beginning to get busy, wine, beer and Pastis being on offer. The youngsters from many miles around were congregating, and there were many surreptitious glances between the girls and boys. The old traditions being played out over again, a chance to meet, an opportunity to flirt; the old, old ritual. The boys were dressed quite casually, but the girls were worthy of note. Some dressed as if going to a ball or a wedding, with skirts of layers of gaudy net, (Ra-Ra skirts my daughter reliably informed me) and a few wearing tiaras and all in bright colours rather as if going to a Spanish *fiesta*.

Another group of slightly older girls, showing a lot of leg and body, with their hair very carefully "messed up" and a great deal of makeup, were being eyed up by the local "Jack the lads," with some anticipation it seemed. Again, the old rituals still up and running!

Well, our family and friends joined in, a bit of socialising, as far as we were able, a bit of dancing and a bit of drinking, and at around midnight, rather like Cinderella, we all crept away back to the caravans. The music was still beating and throbbing for at least two more hours, as I tried to get some sleep. The sounds gradually died away towards four am, I was told, as we sat blearily over our coffee the next morning.

The fete committee workers were already out, or perhaps still there from the previous night, picking up debris from the first nights festivities, and Dave and I took a couple of black bin bags and starting at our end of the square lent a hand, amidst many "Bonjours" and "Merci pour l'assistance" We were now residents, and don't forget the charm offensive, no opportunity should be missed.

Tonight was to be the main event, with the meal, which, we were told would bring many more visitors into the village. About 200 tickets had been sold, as the village barbeque was well known over a large area and this at the time of year when most of France seemed to be "en fete".

The weather was hot and dry, and a large covered tented area had been erected to protect against the heat. Rows and rows of trestle tables and benches had been set up. We had been advised to go over and mark place names on the paper table cloth covering, so that we could be sure of sitting together. Paper plates, serviettes, and plastic cups were provided, but taking your own cutlery and wine glasses was the norm. Well, at 6.30 we were all spruced up again, and ready to party once more. Dave who had returned from a quick tour of the village, reported that two fields, one at each entrance to the village had been marked with signs for car parking, and that cars were pouring in.

Glorious smells of roasting lamb were now rising from the barbeques which had been lit much earlier in the day and set up behind the church. At the little bar we were enjoying glasses of beer and the local Corbieres wine, amidst the general atmosphere of anticipation and excitement. The crowds, at some unperceived signal, started making their way to the eating area and so, clutching our "irons", we followed across the square to take our seats. We were soon being greeted by our new friends, the workers whom we had helped to clear rubbish that morning. A big bunch of very friendly farmers. Now we began to feel like celebrities, what a step change that was. Who says charm offensives won't work.

And so to the meal. First there was the half of a melon with the centre seeds scooped out, and the hole brimming with port, followed by, after a suitable interval, during which the carafes of really decent regional wine had been refilled, the locally made pork pate, great slices of it, served with gherkins and accompanied by baskets of fresh, crusty bread. Absolutely delicious, and we rather pigged out on it. A short while later, amid great cheers and hand clapping the huge platters of meat were carried in by the rosy faced "chefs". Not so much "carved lamb" but meat that had been hacked off the sizzling carcasses. As I write I can almost smell and taste it all over again.

Sunday roast lamb in England would never be the same in the future. For those with mammoth appetites, or even those who perhaps had had a hard week of building work behind them, there were second helpings and we did our best, we were representing England after all. Again, time to refill the by now, empty, wine carafes and a pause to gather ourselves, knowing that there was still cheese and dessert to come. We were also by now looking for the bottles of water strategically placed at intervals along the tables.

The cheese came, not a great affair, almost cheesy triangles, unfortunately not a piece of our favourite Pyrenean sheep's cheese on offer, but later followed by wedges of homemade apple tart, with individual pots of ice cream served alongside. This accompanied by bottles of "bubbly", table banging and cheers.

“The music didn’t stop until 5 am this morning”, grumbled a well hung over son. Dave was also very quiet, and actually so was I. The little ones eyes were rather bleary, and Alex, Tacey and Trish were speaking very quietly and did not seem too lively either. No plates were rattling, or pans clanking, a hush had fallen after the frivolities of the previous night. Digestions also rather delicate after the indiscretions of our over indulgence - Oh yes we would be taking things very easy this morning and just quietly observe the boules in the afternoon.

Boules competitions here in the south of France are very serious affairs indeed and there is a distinct line of difference between the enthusiastic local club player, and those who are there for the prize money. The locals are dressed casually, and carry a piece of towelling to clean the boules between games, whilst the serious players are more flamboyant, and the colour of their towels would appear to have been chosen to match their clothing, with pairs players whether mixed or not, often colour co-ordinated. All players seemed to have the habit of “clicking” their boules together before playing, and the village was ringing with the sound. There is an entry fee, and depending on the numbers of entrants, the prize money could be a very large pot indeed, which is why the very keen players will travel great distances to take part.

So the competition grinds through the dust and heat of the afternoon, with favourites having large and noisy support, leading one to suspect that side betting is also a serious business. The sun is relentless, and the bar is doing a roaring trade, the bottles of beer being served from barrels of iced water. By 5.30 it is clear that the numbers of players have dwindled, with the last pairs left to fight it out.

There is a huge amount of shouting for favourites until finally a huge cheer goes up, and we have the winners who are guided over to a table in the square on which were several very ornate cups. To me they appeared cheap and nasty, but obviously not to the winners and enthusiasts. The envelopes awarded are carefully slipped into a pocket when presented. I can only guess at their values! And so, the fete would play out with more dancing this night and by tomorrow all would be over for another year.

No early activity this Monday morning, but gradually a few people arrived to start the clearing and cleaning up process. We were going to help once more. The little ones had buckets and were collecting stray beer bottles and putting them on the now sadly deserted kiosk. The rest of us with bags picking up rubbish, the music trailer was being stripped and streamers, flags and decorations were being taken down. The farmers and their workers were anxious to return to their late summer and early autumn work programme. The glorious sunflowers were starting to ripen and lower their heads in the heat, and the slower maturing maize was gradually changing colour. The acres of grain land needed to be ploughed again in preparation for the next year's crop and sown in the late autumn and early winter, the annual cycle moves forward once more.

Dave, who was our family's garbage collector, realised that by the end of the morning the village bins would be over flowing, and decided to get rid of our own rubbish first. As always he loaded the wheelbarrow with the bin bags and empty bottles and set off on his circuit of the village. On this circle he would pass a row of small houses at the end of the village. The end one, we understood, belonged to an old fellow and his son, the wife having died some years earlier.

The younger of the two, maybe around fifty years old, drove a lorry for the local agricultural Co-op. A thin, sallow little chap, who was in the habit of wearing light coloured sporting outfits, but at weekends it was coloured tops, light shorts and trainers and with his stature and sparrow like legs, from behind he did resemble two plates stuck together. This had earned him the nickname of SlimBum.

The door of the cottage was what is known as a stable door, in as much as the top and bottom halves opened separately. They also had a dog! This was very similar to the English springer spaniel, a noted gundog, which, whenever someone passed, (when the top part of the door was open), would jump up and down in the air, and bark. You may imagine our remarks about a "springer", we never intentionally provoked him, but we did pass by rather slowly, in order to get the maximum reaction and enjoyment.

One late evening Dave and Trish had set off with the rubbish with the three little girls in tow, and we heard them returning, making loud engine noises, and peeping around the corner we could make out Trish sitting in the wheelbarrow with a torch in each hand, as flashing headlights, amidst much general laughter, just another example of a very happy time.

25 - The Appearance of Beastie

(And a Trial of Strength)

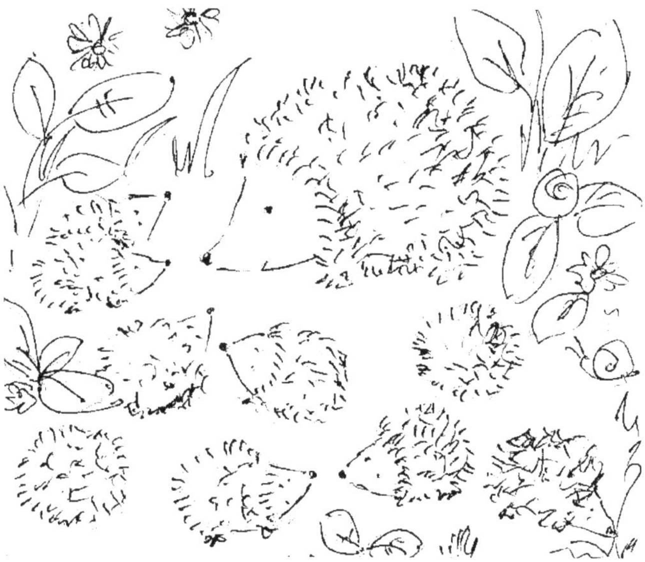

Our good friends Dave and Trish would soon be departing. Their "dropping in" for a couple of days had lasted two weeks and had been of great assistance and also great fun. They would make their journey back through France a leisurely one, to return to prepare again for schools and pick up their lives. We will have two weeks more before our sojourn for this year is finished, and then a mad dash for the port. We still have so much to do.

Dave had finished preparing the lounge window to the courtyard and the first pillars were out of the boxes which were now empty, and awaiting the material for the next lintel to be added. The other box would be made ready for the pillars for upstairs. First, the staircase, all the timber was soon cut to size and length, and the grooves hacked out for the steps and then wacked into place.

When the steps were together we nailed them firmly. It had become a very heavy piece of kit indeed and would certainly do the trick and support the weight of anything we would wish to carry up it. Stone, lintels, timber and all roof materials would eventually test its strength, and Dave was right impressed. A couple of 8x4's (sheets of hardboard) and we had a large working area that could be moved around upstairs as the work required.

That morning on waking as I was lying in bed, listening to nature waking up too, birds, an occasional dog barking away somewhere, a cockerel and even a distant church clock chiming, when some nearer sound became apparent; a sort of snuffling and squeaking that I didn't recognise. I peeped out of the caravan window and realised that it was coming from the other side of the garden wall. I slipped on my shorts and crept quietly over to take a peep.

What a surprise! Here was mummy hedgehog with nine, yes nine juveniles searching and feeding through the dewy grass, a sight I guess, not seen by many. Alex came out after me and we both gazed in amazement, we had never imagined they could have such large broods and considering the harshness of the previous winter she must have found a snug and secure spot to hibernate. I suspected she had crept into an old cellar at the back of the forge and indeed further sleuthing did reveal one cellar with some old straw in the corner of it.

At breakfast talking about the little family, Jon wondered just how hedgehogs managed to breed. I knew the answer, very, very carefully indeed! I was not alone in my nature observations however, as Dave and Trish's smallest girl Charlie, seemed to be absolutely fascinated by creepy crawlies and little creatures.

She had already spotted the entrance to a tiny burrow in the garden. She would kneel, and with infinite patience would twiddle the length of a long piece of grass in the mouth of this burrow and after several minutes a little sniffing and twitching nose appeared – it was a fieldmouse. After a short while studying the grass, the owner of the nose bit the end off and retreated. Charlie showed no surprise but the rest of us were amazed.

This was to become her pet and a daily routine was established, with grass and a grain of rice as a daily feed for the creature, which was soon named Twiddlekins. Charlie spent hours crouching in front of the hole talking to the tiny creature.

But, back to work. Don had told me that a M. Poiret of Castelnaudary had a joinery workshop and would, if contacted, be glad to make two large double glazed units to complete the front of the extension. These would go each side of the centre post, and a wide door would be included on the right hand side to allow good access to the patio area and garden. Cher had already rung him for us, and he would be arriving today to measure and calculate and give us a price. The plan was to place an order now, and he would complete the work through the coming autumn, and install them when ready in order to give the building security and protection during the next winter's weather.

The pillars for the lounge window were now installed, and we would need to complete and secure all downstairs access points before our departure. Dave was upstairs clearing loose stones and rubbish off the wall over the back of the cemetery. Suddenly he shouted, and a small squirrel sized creature shot down the stairs passing me, raced outside and was gone. "What the hell was that?" he said. I had had a better sighting as it flashed by me whilst making its escape, and said that it seemed to be a squirrel type creature, black and white, and with a bottle brush tail.

We were to come across this harmless little chap on many occasions during our years in France. It turned out he was known as a Loir or Edible Dormouse and fairly common in many areas except for Brittany and the Atlantic coast, and who rather liked living in old houses and roofs. Also renowned as a delicacy by the Romans, who, apparently kept them in tall earthenware pots and fattened them on a diet of walnuts. We never felt the inclination to try.

This morning Jon had volunteered to drive to Toulouse in order to collect Dons machine which was now ready. So armed with a cheque he had set off right after breakfast. He was confident he could retrace our steps and would see us later. As Dave and I had already cemented in the pillars to the lounge window, we were discussing the problem of placing the lintel. It was the only lintel we would have to slide into place. It could not be lowered as the wall above was solid.

The danger would be, if care was not taken, that we could end up pushing the window and pillars out into the courtyard. The window itself, as before, had been built in with the pillars, and for added security props were fixed against them from the courtyard side. These would help to hold them in place if we accidently nudged it at all. So, the pillars and window were in place and supported, the lintel was setting in one box, and more pillars in the other box ready for the upstairs.

Dave was carrying decent stone upstairs to continue building up the walls, and I would finish preparing the few remaining support timbers for the floor.

Amongst those that were left was the curved, offending piece that was the cause of the damage to Dons router and which had been cast aside in disgust after the event. It had not improved in shape since the last time, and I placed it on the workbench so as to power plane the lower edges off. I was going to have to guide the plane with one hand whilst holding the wood firmly with the other. I completed one side successfully, turned it over to do the other and had got part way along when calamity occurred. The weight of the plane on the twisted timber caused it to turn, putting my hand in line with the cutting blade, which shot forward cutting a groove in my hand as a consequence.

Dave heard the resulting commotion and rushed downstairs to find me clutching my wrist and with blood dripping onto the floor. So to the first aid station, sitting at the table with a bowl of warm water with a drop of Dettol in it, cleaning the wound and assessing the damage. "Hmm", said Dave, quite used to dealing with field injuries, "nice tidy groove, no flaps of skin, healing cream, bind tightly and dress daily". So a very awkward piece of wood had come back to haunt me once more, and on the very day that Jon was collecting the machine that it had damaged the last time.

The work for me that day was over, the bleeding had eased but the hand needed to be rested for 24 hours, and then possibly, after redressing and wearing a glove, I could resume a little activity. It was the left hand I had damaged and as I was right handed all was not lost. Jon arrived back from Toulouse with Dons machine and the repair just about passed muster. It didn't look that pretty but it was strongly pinned and repaired and would work. I hoped that Don would look at it in the same way, so it was with some trepidation that I went to return it.

He came to the door, took the machine from me and commented that, as no new part could be found for it, it was probably the best that could be achieved. I just apologised once more and that chapter was now closed. The reaction I received from Jon over the damage to my hand was predictable. He couldn't believe that I would have tried to use that particular piece of wood again, and called me all the appropriate names possible, finishing up with the usual "old Cornish farmer" bit, which, of course refers to the "nothing to be wasted" adage.

My hand, the next day, was not looking at all bad, a quite deep cut, but clean, and after treating again with the cream, covered and plastered, and into a fresh glove, I was up for anything again. The lintel of the lounge window had come out of its box well, and now came the problem of getting it into place. With Dave on one end and I on the other we hefted it off its props on the floor, to assess its weight. My guess was 2 hundredweight, my old farmer's measure, Dave reckoned more than 200 pounds: this was not going to be easy.

Normally one would have the assistance of jacks or mechanical hoists to lift the lintel into position. Unfortunately we did not have this type of help. Instead, someone would have to squat half bent in the window to achieve this. "Well" said Dave "if we build two supports, one at each side of the window, and put the lintel on them, in theory all we have to do is to lift forward and then down". I had also decided that this would be the only practical way, but... then Dave said that because of my back and hand, "I guess it's me then". I smiled ruefully, and thought that with Jon offering help on one corner and me on the other we stood a good chance of success.

We built the temporary supports and I checked the props in the courtyard to make sure they were holding firm, and then the three of us lifted it bodily onto those two supports. Well that went well enough, so now for the hard bit. It was not easy for Dave to get himself balanced but after some fractional moves and adjustments he was in position in the window. He said "When I say NOW I'm going to take the weight off the supports, you two then assist with the lift and we can move it forward into place.

Ok, NOW", he heaved, he had the weight; we added muscle power and moved it forward into its position. Bingo! It was resting firmly in its place. We helped him down and gave ourselves a handclap and slaps on the shoulder. It really had been a hard physical and engineering achievement.

26 - The Big Stink Solution

It was decided that after this effort, we had earned ourselves a day off and after much discussion and consulting maps a two family trip was agreed. We sorted out a route which would take us to Foix, which we understood was well worth visiting. Foix had long been an important town, known as the gateway to the Pyrenees, and because of its position had been the focal point in many conflicts over centuries, as being a refuge for Cathars as well as a route for World War II pilots fleeing the Nazis.

We would travel "entourage" and find an appropriate site along the way to have a picnic lunch. We thought that we would head to Mirepoix and then on to Lavelanet, a route which would skirt the lower Pyrenees and approach Foix from the south; a round trip, with the shorter route for our return.

Dave and I, when discussing this outing, and knowing that a visit to the castle at Foix would give us a bird's eye view over the roofs of the town, had another reason for being keen on this visit. With the pressure from two families upon the drainage of our little cottage, a certain miasma was beginning to hover over the site, especially in the mornings! We were going to take the opportunity to research stench pipes!

We had realised during our previous travels around France in those days that problems of sewage and waste water didn't appear to be dealt with in the same manner as in England! We did feel, however, that if we were able to cast our eyes over the roofs over of this city we might get some indication of the position, size, height and shape of those pipes that were now coming into use. Naturally we hadn't revealed our plan to the rest of our families.

Foix was in the department of the Ariege and was reported to have considerable connections with the Cathar movement of the 12th and 13th centuries, a topic that had long had a fascination for Alex and I. Also cropping up, once more, was the name of our old friend Simon De Montfort, leader of the Albigensian crusade and who had by now for us achieved the reputation of being the greatest murderer and thug to be found in this part of France. All in the name of religion! Having found this name cropping up over many years, we came to realise that his was a dynasty and all the family, many of the same name, weren't all bad. This Simon was not to be confused with Simon 6th of that name who helped to found parliamentary democracy in England, and had a university named after him. There had been so many changes throughout history involving this family.

The Ariege has areas of great fertility, gorges with icy cold water descending from the winter snow falls, and through its higher reaches the soil thins and the terrain becomes bleaker as one climbs to the mountains beyond. The drive was glorious through these valleys and the weather was clear and dry, and there were few other cars to bother us. After a coffee stop and then a wind through yet another gorge, we were looking for a picnic area. We were driving alongside a river and an opportunity soon occurred close to a bridge, and we were soon ensconced with tables, food and drink, with a view looking across the bridge.

There was a small village on the other side facing a wide river bed, which at this time of the year did not have too much water, but flowing quite quickly under the bridge, which must have been two hundred metres long. In the middle of this bridge there appeared to be huts or cabins clinging to its side and we decided we would stroll over and examine these strange structures after lunch.

After eating, most of us stretched out on the ground in the sun, but Jon, along with the girls wandered out across the bridge. There was a short delay for examination, and then we heard peals of laughter from them, they were pointing and holding their sides with mirth and beckoning for the rest of us to join them.

We soon arrived and would you believe it, this had been the local community's public loo! Complete with constant running water. A row of six one holers, all in a line and the thought of them sitting there discussing the local news was just the funniest thing. Remarks such as, this must have been fun in the plum season, followed, and then, all still giggling, we returned to our cars and continued with our trip on to Foix and its huge castle.

Its appearance was sudden and dramatic and arriving from the northern side down around a bend up on our left it majestically appeared. Powerful, huge, glowing in the sun, it dominated the landscape. Strategically situated to control the area and defend its inhabitants.

On arrival at the car park of the castle, there were some summer visitors about, but it was not difficult to find parking spaces, and we walked across to the entrance and ticket office without delay. As with most Historical sites in France, entry was not expensive and we were soon inside, examining maps and plans and deciding how and what to see as there was so much. The walkway along the castle wall with its views over the city would be amazing and would give Dave and I the results of the research we were after. The vision of the city from this height was indeed stunning and one could well imagine how difficult it would have been to breach this castle and overthrow the defenders of such massive fortifications.

The youngsters were dashing hither and thither and soon saying. “Seen that, been there” as is their way. We had agreed to meet up at some seats in the centre of the keep and a short discussion followed as to what we had seen and in some cases what we had missed!

Dave and I had finished our roof gazing efforts and were comparing notes on types of stench pipes observed. We had agreed that very few had been spotted, but their normal height would be above roof level, and their diameters, unusually small, at about 5 centimetres seemed to be the norm, and I would adopt that for our system when the waste plumbing advanced to the upstairs bathroom.

The return route, as planned, was a good deal shorter and in the heat we were all happy to get back to the “homestead” and the promise of cold beer and barbeques.

27 - Peyra, A Neighbouring Village Fete

The walls upstairs could now be brought up to roof height, and the window lintels prepared and completed. It was important to begin to think of the security of the cottage until we returned next year. M. Poiret had been and measured and had agreed to make and erect the large glass front of the extension that autumn to complete its security.

The front door aperture also had to be secured temporarily unless a new front door could be purchased, as had the downstairs windows before our departure. Jon would soon fashion the shutters, and I, after making good the stonework around the windows, and completing the back cemetery wall would then point the walls of the hall and kitchen diner.

My word, it was hot, closer to 40°C I guessed, as we gathered to set off for the fete and feast at the neighbouring village, Peyra sur l'Hers. We had enjoyed our own village's festivities so much that we had decided to join in with another one. Cars had already started parking on the verges approaching the village by the time we arrived, but we spotted a couple of gaps for ours and strolled on into the village.

The whole place was festooned with great garlands of streamers and bunting, obviously the residents had spent hours of work decorating their village, and we could already hear music and sounds of activity ahead we were now joining a stream of people moving towards the square. Here, tables were laid out in long rows, and we quickly commandeered a block and placed our cutlery and glasses to secure our seats.

None of us were familiar with this village and it certainly had more life than ours and was large enough to support a bakery at least! There was a large religious retreat at the far end of the village, gated, and the doors and shutters firmly secure against the frivolity outside; I didn't expect those residents would be joining us this evening.

At this point a big hand bell was being rung, calling us all to the table, as the feast was about to start. The menu was very similar to that of last weeks, which pleased our entire group, but the lamb was a touch rare for our little ones' taste and their portions were quickly wrapped in serviettes to be used on our BBQ tomorrow. Waste not Want not!

There was a large family seated on our right headed by a smiling, middle aged man who left his place and came over to us and introduced himself as the Maire, he then pointed to each member of his family with an introduction. We of course reciprocated. He then said in an educated French voice, which we had no problem understanding, "you are the English who are renovating the cottage", to which I replied in the vernacular "Mais Weh (oui)". He raised a glass to us in welcome as did his family, we toasted each other, it was a very special moment.

I noticed both Jon and Tacey taking a special interest in his teenage daughter and later spotted them chatting together. Brilliant!

The sun was setting now and it was slowly getting dark, and many lights came on in the square as we finished our cheeses and desserts. Then the coffee and bubbly arrived with much noise and fanfare. Toasts were given and new friendships sealed, what a splendid evening! A short speech by Monsieur le Maire thanking those who had worked so hard for the event and then he said "maintenent les artifices".

Amid much whistling the lights went out and the first rocket was launched high into the air over the village. Much oohing and ahhing, and then the explosion which spread its beauty over us in a large umbrella of colour.

The firework display continued for some time and we speculated as to its cost. We couldn't see that it could come out of the meal price, which was very reasonable. Perhaps it came from central funds. We did know that local councils in France had control over a larger percentage of their taxes; perhaps the funding came from there. After the final crescendo we made our way back to our cars, chattering about the evening and comparing the two village meals, commenting on how much more welcoming their maire had been, and how much we had enjoyed the fireworks.

After the short drive back we all turned in, and the next morning I could hear that our friends were preparing for their early departure. We rose quietly, greeted each other and had our breakfast as they continued with their last packing.

Our car was moved out of the garden and Dave reversed his back to hook up to his caravan, and then slowly drew out into the square where he parked so we could make our final farewells. Charlie was saying 'au revoir' to her little furry friend, and with kisses and handshakes being given and received they then got into the car and slowly drove across the square, and their visit for this year was over. We would miss them.

The quiet that then descended was marked and palpable, and a large brown space on the grass that their van and awning had left would remind us of the pleasure that their company, and Dave's assistance had given us on this visit. So many laughs and memories of these moments of effort and pleasure would stay with us for the rest of our lives. Ah well, that was then, this is now and we have two weeks left to complete this year's programme.

Outside, the gutter had to be placed over and above the cemetery wall. I would also like to stone edge the patio area, which would spread from the glass garden door that M. Poiret would be building, and then also cast steps down to form an entrance to the garden. Jon would roll over all the larger stones from those left by the garden wall, clearing them out of the way and over to where I would be needing them. I would fix the gutter above the wall of the cemetery first.

The supports were soon in place, a metre apart, firmly fixed to the ends of the support timbers of the roof. Slotting and fixing the gutter and starting at the top end, the run was soon installed and looking good. Having included a blank at the top to contain the water flow and also an angle turned into the garden at the other end, all sections were clipped and checked, and I stood back in the cemetery to view it.

The Maire had asked me to keep it well back from the cemetery and this I had done, to a degree, but not further than the centre of the guttering. If after a violent thunderstorm the volume of water overflowed the gutter it would end up in the graveyard but not compromise the building. This was my concession and was as far as I was prepared to go. It looked natural and the size was appropriate for the length of the roof.

Meanwhile Jon had managed to roll about a dozen big stones to points convenient to the patio area. Together we then started to dig the shallow trench into which they would be placed, upright and with their best faces to the garden.

The position of the steps, numbering three, had been decided and cut out squarely. Jon found some timber and prepared the shuttering for the first step and then we were ready for a large mix of cement. He would fill the shuttering and keep me supplied with cement for the retaining wall.

We took a coffee break and stood back and looked at our effort, Alex and Tacey came to admire and comment and we all agreed that the patio would be big enough for lounging and dining when complete. Such imagination we all had!

We were obviously very busy but it was so quiet after the departure of our friends, it was going to take some days to become used to their absence. To complete the steps would take a few days because of cement drying time, but the stonework of the wall was finished comfortably by the end of that working day.

28 - We Eat with the Locals

(And Buy a Door)

Pointing stonework is a slow three part operation, but the beauty of old stone makes it aesthetically very satisfying. To begin with, we cleaned the wall with a stiff brush and scratched out all existing loose material, and then liberally filled the joints with a malleable mix of equal parts of white cement, lime and sand, with sufficient dye to achieve the colour we required.

Because the weather was very warm, we had to dampen the joints with a fine spray of water to aid adhesion, and left it touch dry. We then had to carefully brush off any surplus, before we could stand back to admire the result. This is by far the most satisfying moment of the entire operation as the stone colours were displayed to their natural best.

The following evening we were eating at Evelyn and Pauls; they were the nearest farmers to the village whom we had befriended, after an introduction by Cher at the fete. Evelyn's sister and brother in law lived at the other end of the village, he drove a local milk collection lorry and they had two youngsters, about Jon's age and were also friendly with the Mayor of Peyras' daughter.

This would lead to a bit of socialising for Jon and to a meeting with their cousin called Crystelle. I believe there was a little holiday romance, and he still speaks with fondness about it. So it looks as if he is on a charm offensive as well!

The meal with Evelyn and Paul, which included Tacey and Jon, was a great success; the language problem seemed not so bad after several glasses of wine, (which is well known as great help to ones French), It was a splendid meal and a most pleasant evening. Alex and Evelyn talked food, food, food for the whole evening, no change there then, and Alex came away with the ONLY and ORIGINAL recipe for Cassoulet of the

South West of France: That of Castelnaudary – all others being poor replicas.

I thoroughly enjoyed talking agriculture with Paul, who had been unaware of my background in farming. We discussed the differences, caused by the variations in their climate and that of the South West of England, which reflected not only on their crops but on their stock management as well, with their animal's being housed through the hot dry summer months.

Jon had been invited to a birthday party some miles away, the following weekend, and would be collected on the Saturday morning and after a sleep over, return on the Sunday evening. Great, good to see the young gathering as always and we were very happy for him.

Whilst at the meal with Evelyn and Paul we discovered that our little house had, for many generations been owned by Pauls family, they also believed that the house fire that was evident had occurred at sometime in the 1800's and that it had been started by the Maires wife's grandfather because the family had been throwing their garbage over the wall onto their family tomb. This then, could be the reason why there had been so much opposition to our renovation. It could have been coming through his wife's mother. Who said we can't learn from history.

Front doors in France are always solid and decorative and we needed one. After discussing at length with Don it seemed that a trip once more to the commercial estates in Toulouse would give us the best choice. There were two huge Meneuserie outlets on this side of the city that he knew of. So we all decided to go and search.

These doors would, of course, form another part of the winter security and we would need time to install it. We took a cool box with bread, ham, fruit and cold drinks with us, and set off after breakfast.

A day out, how exciting to go shopping for a door, (the family said), as we marvelled at how quiet this road was. We were travelling along the N road through avenues of huge poplars, which were now so familiar to us.

As the heat rose, we blessed Napoleons initiative in having them planted in order to provide shade for his troops as they marched. Just as that fact was being discussed by the family we spotted a troop of legionnaires ahead. In Dave's terms they were "yomping" or running in columns. One soldier was slightly behind the others, and seemed to be suffering from the pace, he looked hellish - sweat through the back and front of his shirt and over his face, and then, as we accelerated past him he started yelling "Brit, Brit" waving wildly, it gave us all such a shock as it was so unexpected. Jon asked "are you going to stop dad?" and I replied "of course not, he will have joined for a very good reason". What had made him take such an extreme decision in the first place we wondered, which gave rise to many speculations, and without answers. A sombre mood descended on us as we reflected on what we had just witnessed. Anyway, I said, with this haircut they may have thought that I was a deserter!

Not helping our mood, the sunflowers were now beginning to look rather sad, with their heads slowly drooping, and we all agreed that it reminded us that this was a sure sign that it was nearly time to return home. There were a few villages on this route to Toulouse and views of others on each side of the canal, farther away in the distance; many had beautiful church towers, supporting one or two visible bells. This gave echoes of ancient Spanish and Moorish architectural influence, and I had seen films set in Mexico with these same features.

The canal was the Canal du Midi which wandered the valley from Toulouse until it eventually met the Mediterranean at Sete. This area had seen so much change and disruption through wars and unrest for thousands of years. Now, however, having served the purpose for transporting goods, it was being used mainly for leisure, with many holiday makers taking barge holidays. Meandering slowly through this beautiful countryside is idyllic, with its history, robust wine, luscious summer fruits and rustic country food.

On the left just ahead a commercial estate hove into view, and Don had said that if we looked for a big sign LaPeyre they had a huge department, stocking doors, windows and staircases. We would start there, and armed with the measurements and a tape measure, we entered and soon found the right department. There was a large number to choose from, and our first exercise would be to select a few which would be suitable for the front door of our cottage.

After some time we had found four that would be fine. They all measured the same and so would fit, so now it was down to the price. All of them were really well made of exotic hard wood. They were all expensive of course, but considering their quality, not bad value and with no great differences in their price. This door is a focal point I said to Alex, you choose, and after a little discussion, she did just that. After paying, an assistant carried it out to the car and we loaded and made it secure on the roof rack, and were soon on our way back down the road.

At the earliest opportunity we turned off, we were looking for a point of access to the bank of the canal to have our picnic, and very soon we found it, and had the rug out and were surrounded by our victuals. The canal seemed not to be moving at all, sluggish and not very inviting. Jon wondered if anyone would swim in it and we all doubted it. "Would you?" Jon asked his sister "certainly not" she replied, It was almost green, and being August did not smell too good either.

The air was heavy, and the girls were soon putting on protection against possible mosquito bites. The foliage was looking dusty and sun soaked and needed a refreshing thunderstorm to cheer it up, but the cicadas were ever busy. It is so strange that after two or three weeks of their sound constantly in the background that one has now to concentrate to hear them. The picnic was great, and Alex's choice of cheese and wonderful tomatoes, radish and fresh salad, with newly baked bread, was perfect for the stop and we were soon continuing on our way.

The door fitted beautifully, the measurements proved to be very accurate and with only a small amount of stone chiselling, it slotted into place. We only had to drill the frame of the door to mark its final position, put the plugs in the stonework and screw back tightly. A small line of cement around the frame to finish the work and to prevent draught and insect ingress and the job was complete.

We all stood out in the square to admire the transformation, and it was now so easy to imagine the house with the roof on, how smart is that! Whilst finishing the cemetery wall in the garden by the patio, and then the pointing of the wall in the lounge leading to the hall, my thoughts were on what would be needed for this project next year when we returned. There was a kitchen to be built in, the boiler to be plumbed for hot water, and a permanent inspection cover for the fosse septique, were just a few of items to be prioritised.

I digress; finishing the skimming of the wall containing the bathroom would bring the work in this part of the building to a conclusion. If there was time this year I would like to put in place the supports for a proper outdoor BBQ for our use next year when we returned. It would be placed by the entrance of the home of the little furry friend of the children. I had assured them before we left that she had store of rice and seeds for another winter and would be fine.

So this wonderful working holiday was drawing to a close, and the entire family were as brown as the proverbial berries, and none of them now wondered what on earth I had purchased. We all realised that another years effort similar to this one would produce a very attractive holiday home, maybe a little isolated, but exactly what one group of holiday makers would look for. Walking and hiking in these hills, bird watching and history gathering would be ideal for those trying to escape the roaring crowd that many resorts attracted and was one of its attributes and would not be a drawback.

Jon's party had been great fun, he said, and Crystelle would be visiting her cousin again next week to attend other fetes in this area, and he hoped he would be able to go. Tacey was returning to university on our return and was happy to have had a long, lazy summer reading, tanning and storing up energy. Her renewed relationship with Trish and the three little girls had been very fulfilling for all of them, and she had done more than her fair share of the catering. Jon then raised the question of the use of the car, and we were both rather reticent as our return would be quite soon. As it turned out the other families took turns in providing the transport, so he used ours only once, which was fine.

29 - We Return to our Other Life

Eventually the day for our departure arrived, and after the final packing and photographing our achievements of the summer, we hitched up the caravan, wound up the legs and drove out of the garden. Quite a sad moment in many ways, Bye, bye little house, we will see you again next year.

Through the square, we stopped at Don and Cher's door for a final farewell and then crept slowly away. Jon blew his usual raspberry as we passed the maire's house as he did again when we passed Mr Bricolage in Castelnaudary. He actually blew raspberries at every Bricolage in France on that journey.

The traffic became heavier after we passed Toulouse - it seemed that everybody in Europe had finished their holiday. Indeed in one service area, (as it was lunchtime and having left the autoroute), we could not find a space for our car and caravan to park, and so a very hairy re-entry to the autoroute followed. Fortunately as we drove further away from the south the traffic eased a little and we found stopping and parking further up in France much simpler.

At one of these stops we were talking to another returning British family, who had been listening to their car radio, who said there were problems at the ports. Apparently French farmers were blocking all accesses in protest against British meat imports. The dad of that family was expected back at work in three days and had already decided to head for Zeebrugge.

When asked if I would do the same, I said "Zeebrugge? Bugger Zeebrugge!" (which later became a family motto) so you can assume reader that we would be going via Cherbourg if at all possible. There were road blocks on the autoroute, and at one stage, in Northern France, we were diverted but were finally able to make our way and departed as planned from the port of Cherbourg to Weymouth.

Our progress continued through Dorset and onto the A30 to Honiton, and then onwards to Exeter and the Cornwall and Devon border which we called Home.

As we picked up the threads of our working lives there, our thoughts would often turn to what would lie before us on our next visit to the village. Dave had said, before his departure, that he would love to be a part of the team, to help put the main roof on the cottage. Without doubt, with the size of timbers in mind, hard work it would be, and I could think of no one better to help me achieve this.

I had another friend, an electrician, who had remarked casually that he would love just a few days away and would be happy to finish up the small amount of wiring which was still to be done in the cottage. Sam and Martin, university friends of Alex, were also most anxious to discover what we were doing in the South West of France.

It didn't look as if we were to be short of visitors in the coming year. Some six weeks later, we heard from Cher, that all was well, but that they had sold their house, which came as a great surprise to us. The purchasers were called Mr and Mrs Pegg who would be holiday letting the studio which would be very handy for overflow friends and family we thought, and immediately furnished Sam and Martin with their details.

30 – All Preparations Made

(But Another Passenger Included...)

It was important to book early for the journey for the peak holiday period - particularly as we were keen to take advantage of every day of Alex's summer break. We had already started accumulating the items that would be needed for our project, the fosse inspection cover, much more sophisticated than the French equivalent, kitchen worktops and flat packed units were already loaded inside the caravan.

Thought now had to be put to our travel arrangements: Tacey would be joining us later this year as she would be in transition from university to a job at Friends Provident and Mum(in law) having realised this, had decided that she could travel with us in her place. So we were still four, she had added that she would sleep fine in the awning, quite determined not to be left out.

I had the measurements of the upstairs of the cottage, and was playing around with the area on paper. We already had a staircase installed which arrived upstairs passing a window on the left looking over the churchyard, and directly ahead was a small picture window, facing the back of the church, which gave light to that area. There was another window at the front with a view across the square.

The upstairs space was more than adequate for two double bedrooms and toilet facilities, but the puzzle was how to fit it all in, without having to pass through one bedroom to gain access to the other.

We had in stock a toilet, bidet and hand basin and it would be ideal not to have to come down the stairs and possibly disturb other sleepers whilst on a comfort tour. A small hall against the back wall would solve the privacy part, but the space lost would convert one bedroom into a single immediately. Then it occurred to me that if I created a small "Jack and Jill" bathroom against the opposite wall and with a lockable door at each side which would allow access from both bedrooms. This small bathroom was actually a toilet and wash room, but also a passage between the two. How ingenious is that! I would really enjoy seeing it installed and plumbed this coming summer. So these plans were being made during the period of that winter and into the spring. In no time at all we would be making that journey once more.

The spring that year was late, and it really was nearly June before the weather started to improve, as it decided to launch into a mediocre British summer once more. The plans for this seasons work were well advanced, and we would be picking Alex up at school on the day her term finished, and head to port.

The crossing was early the following day and we decided to sleep in the caravan at the port the night before. Mum would be collected the day before we left home, and Jon, who had been to Australia, was already home and rearing to go, with thoughts of Crystelle perhaps?

The time from June to the last week of July sped past, and here we were collecting Alex. A couple of the mothers and their offspring, (who were still at the school gate), waved us goodbye as we pulled up the road. Hurrah!

On arrival at the port, we tucked ourselves away in a corner of the car park and settled down for the night. There was not to be too much sleep at the port for the four of us, due to the constant arrival of other travellers but the night passed and we were soon crossing the channel.

The route down through France was by now becoming familiar, and we made excellent towing progress. We had already planned to rest up the second night at a service station, which meant parking the caravan in that area for overnighting lorries. There was a slight drawback to this arrangement as the engines of refrigerated lorries start up at various times of the night in order to keep their chillers and temperatures to a set level, and sadly when they started up everyone was disturbed. We would arrive tired but not downhearted

31 - We Arrive to No Fanfare

(Or Welcome!)

As we drove through Castelnaudary we pointed out features of the town, and various outlets for provision purchases and materials to Mum. She was enjoying the drive and the scenery as we climbed slowly up towards the village. She remarked on how different the landscape was here to her beloved Dordogne.

As we drew through the narrows to the square there was no bunting of welcome, no fanfare at all, and very quiet this late July afternoon. A solitary car was parked outside the house that was now the Pegg's, and our little cottage looked quite sad and neglected at the end of the square. We were so keen to see the result of the work of M. Poiret at the front of the extension toward the garden, and we knew that the keys had been left by Don with the Pegg's.

The garden as expected had the annual overgrowth to attend to, but evidence of the caravans and awnings from last year were still to be seen. This year at least we knew there were no stones or rubbish in the way, and that my knee was not damaged, and I was able to offer a full contribution to the effort of cutting and clearing.

The front glasswork and door looked splendid, double glazed and perfect in every way. Jon volunteered to go over and introduce himself and collect the keys from the Pegg's and on his return, after opening up the front door said that the Pegg's were amiable and had invited Alex and Mum over for a cup of tea. Great, I said, you can do that while we are preparing the garden but before you go we'll have a look around inside.

The extension was dry and relatively dust free, but the roofless cottage showed evidence that it had been open to the elements. There was reason to think that someone had been regularly to the patio area and Alex heard later from the Peggs that dear old M Papy (owner of the old forge) used to bring a folding chair and just sit there in the sun, admiring the view and, probably remembering the years past when he worked for his customers next door at the forge.

It was not hard to imagine the horses tied at the front, waiting for shoeing, and carts and machines for mending and adaption to the new methods, and the smell of the burning coke, and the ring of his hammer on iron. So much change he had seen over those years, in peace time, both before and after the war. He like many others had gone to fight and returned having lost the sight of an eye. He was very self conscious of it as he wore no patch, and would cover it with his hand when he talked to you, oh so very quietly. A sudden thought crossed my mind that perhaps he was guarding the cottage for us from any possible arson attack, knowing more of the history than we did! Ah well all just speculation, but now back to the present.

The mower was already unloaded, and we would get the area tidy in no time, and be able to get the caravan set up, with the legs down and awning up. Very much in the same position as last year asked Jon; yes I think we had that about right I said. We needed to leave room for Dave's van, which we knew was following, and would be with us in two days. Garden cleared, caravan parked, awning up, all just like clockwork.

Whilst all this was going on Alex and Mum had been over to the Pegg's for the cup of tea. The Pegg's, they said, were charming, and that he was recovering from a long illness. They were amazed how quickly we had got ourselves organised. The picnic table and chairs were in the garden and all items that had been stored in the caravan and car were unloaded and taken into the "kitchen". Jon switched on the electricity and the water so we were up and running.

The two small caravan fridges were plugged in, and Mums frame bed put up in the awning ready for her to attend to. Such organisation! Alex and Mum now turned their attention to the evening meal. Quite simple, she said, just what we have brought with us, well that can't be complicated can it? A big shop for stock and fresh foods tomorrow, she said, and could Jon drive us to Castelnaudary? No problem, I said, I need to reassess the work here, and get my head around the programme of the work which would start with the roof.

Dave's time with us on this visit is a bit more limited, and I aim to finish the roof in approximately a week, achievable I think. I uncovered the heavy timbers, five, and the big wall plates, two, all present and correct. There were many lengths of 5x4 suitable for both the roof and the partitions of the bathroom walls. The measuring and cutting of these beams would be done on trestles, but the rest would be cut and handed up to the roof from what would become the lounge.

So one of the first jobs would be moving that stack into the cottage ready to be cut and prepared. We had decided that the flat packed units and kitchen worktops would have to be stored carefully out of the way indoors. We would need a visit to LePeyne for various other kitchen items in due course. In the meantime to serve as temporary shelving, three rows of blocks stacked three high, with floorboards across with two layers would work very well. Almost like the real thing, said Alex... such imagination!

Amongst the items brought for use down here was a 'built-in' BBQ set, this would be placed into the stonework base we had built at the end of last year. This would give us more space in the garden and offer the opportunity for both families to use it when fired and ready.

The new clothes line had also been brought out and been strung from tree to tree, the shower hose and slats were again in place, but we expected the proper shower cabinet to be plumbed and serviceable very soon.

My friend, Hurd (but never seen) would be with us next week and this would be part of his effort during his stay. He had earned that title by not turning up for a job on one occasion in England. He had a contract with the regional Hospitals to be on call in case of electrical emergencies, and had been diverted and the name had stuck!

The rest of the materials for the roof were identified, the battens and felt were there and ready, so we could make a good start tomorrow. We were all relieved and happy to be here.

The weather was hot and dry and promised a good spell for some time.

32 - Mum Mightily Impressed

Mum was fascinated and excited by the cottage but I wondered what her attitude would have been had she seen it last year in its original condition. She was a great sun lover, so this weather would suit her very well.

We all slept well after the long and tiring journey but were up next morning bright and early. Mum had already been to the bathroom, had a wash in a large bowl and was dressed ready for the day. She was enjoying the early morning air and was watching the feeding frenzy of the swifts, swallows and housemartins. After greeting me she said that she could not hear a thing, no cars, lorries, planes - not even an engine, what a treat it was to be here. Her enthusiasm was a pleasure to hear, and I knew she didn't mind roughing it a bit. She would embrace it and enjoy every minute.

Breakfast over, and when Jon, Alex and Mum had left for the supermarket I installed and fitted the new BBQ into the stonework. I was amused and happy to note that Twiddlekins was evidently still very much in residence. Dave's little'uns would be so happy to find that she had wintered well.

To move the 5x4 timbers into the cottage would take a little while, but it would be sensible to get them out of the garden before Dave and family arrived, and would also increase the space we had. The battens could remain there, covered, for the moment; we would use them bundle by bundle, as we needed them.

The idea was, that after the process of getting the beams up into place, and the support timbers on them, it would enable us to fill between them with stone and cement, and at the same time make the walls complete and flush to the timbers. Much easier to do it that way around than struggling to complete the walls after the roof was on, so careful preparations were a must, with list to be taken to Tangios to buy the things we would need.

There was some cement left from last year and still plenty of sand, but organising materials ahead was good planning - perhaps we would get to tile our patio area this year and if so with what?

All these questions must be considered now to keep the progress flowing. Dave and Un-Hurd would be gone after a couple of weeks, but other friends would be arriving and a forward plan would be necessary once more, to line up a very busy summer.

The family arrived back from shopping with food, drink and general provisions, and began to unpack the car and store things away in the “kitchen” using the side door in the courtyard. Jon and I decided to cement the permanent sewage cover in place at the bottom of the garden steps, as we needed no crises or accidents this year, and we placed a guard around it until the cement had dried.

We then turned our attention to the main timbers for the roof; with a long tape we measured the apex, and the other measurements between the two walls to confirm the length needed for these huge beams. Sufficient extra length had to be added so as to gain good support on the walls and obviously we could not assume that they were parallel with such an old building.

Jon and I then lifted the first timber onto the trestles to mark and then cut, took a deep breath before lifting, and Jon said “and you think this will be on top of the cottage this week?”. These timbers were 20 centimetres square and over four metres long. “Oh yes” I said with a smile.

It took us ages with a hand saw to cut these timbers to length, but as I remarked to Jon they will be lighter when their ends are cut off. We heard a toot of a car horn, announcing that Dave and family had arrived, and we all gathered round to greet them. They were surprised and delighted to see Mum with us, as they had known her for many years.

After reversing in and setting up, he was very quickly casting his eyes over M. Poirets work and then, after visiting the toilet, had glanced through to admire the new front door. Coming back out he came down the completed steps into the garden. The new inspection cover looked good, and he was very impressed with the permanent BBQ. The wall around the front of the patio had started to weather already and he admired that as well. “My!” He said “You two were busy after we left last year.”

His girls were already on their knees, hoping to attract little furry beast, to be sure that it was still in habitation and OK; there were great shrieks from them when it was briefly spotted.

It was as if we had never left. Quite magical. A cold beer or two were cracked that night as we shared our meal, and discussed the world, our families, the weather and the programme for the next few days.

Dave had already examined, and lifted the end of one beam which had been on the trestles; he just gave me a speculative glance, and I gave a little nod. Tomorrow was going to be quite a challenge, would we be up to it, or would we be appealing to Paul our friendly farmer for a front end loader on a large tractor? By tomorrow night we would know the answer to that question.

33 - Heavy and High; the Roof

We were a bit like professional weightlifters the next morning, me with my back support and Dave doing stretching exercises at the wall. As a show I was strutting over and back, as they do to summon up all the Gods of strength. We all laughed.

The scaffold had already been placed at the front of the cottage on the left hand side, and the extension ladder was ready on the right hand side. When we carried the beam up to the front of the cottage Jon would move the trestles ready to receive it once more. “Let’s call this the heavy weight shuffle” I said, as we sat gasping after this initial effort. Dave, bless him, said, “That at least in the next operation we do not have to support that weight for so long”.

Having caught our breath we considered the next move. This was the beam for the far side of the cottage; we did not fancy lifting it over the Apex timber. The three of us would lift one end up onto the scaffold, and then the other end would be lifted up the ladder, step by step.

We had already discussed this situation once before, and agreed that Dave’s legs were stronger than mine, but that my arms were stronger than his, therefore Dave said he would take the first one up the ladder. I agreed, I would steady and support the timber on the scaffold and Jon would hold the bottom of the ladder. So fine, we were organised.

The end of the timber having been firmly placed on the scaffold, Jon and I lifted the other end, and Dave stepped behind it and taking the weight, with our help, mounted the bottom rung, with his legs bent he now rested it on his thighs. “How‘s it feel Dave?” I enquired cautiously. “Heavy but good and safe”, he said.

So we lifted with him and he moved up and up to the fifth step, which was then out of reach for any more assistance from us. There would be five more steps to go before he reached the top of the wall. I then got up on the scaffold, and Jon attended to the safety of Dave’s ladder. Lifting the other end I said “in your own time Dave” he flexed his muscles and heaved, and mounted another rung.

This procedure continued until the top of the wall was in reach. Then Dave said “the next effort has to be as one” and I said OK. “Together”, I shouted “One, Two, Three, HEAVE!” and with this last big effort it was up on the wall and secure. We rested for a moment and then I said “we would be safer, I think, if we mounted the wall and walked this timber up and over the apex and to its resting place and then later following it with the apex timber”.

We both hopped up onto the alternate walls, and rolling it slowly we moved it up to the apex, and then down to its permanent situation on the other side. Standing to admire the different views we had, we heard a slow handclap coming from the garden and we both bowed. This procedure was repeated twice more, and I took my turn mounting the ladder with the second, and in what seemed little time, the main beams were up and in place.

Dave and Trish were going shopping that afternoon, and Jon and I would get the wall plates in place, and start preparing the purloins, which would be the next stage of the operation.

The roof was somewhat like a sandwich, first the purloins, with two edges planed, and quarter rounds panel pinned to their inside edges to support the plaster board, which was supplied, coloured in white on the underside, we had already cut them to fit the sections and to rest on those quarter rounds.

The support timbers would be placed at forty centimetres apart, the same width as the insulation rolls, which would be unwound onto the plasterboard. Then sawn timber boards would cover the top and would be firmly nailed before the tarred roofing felt, battens and lastly the tiles would be added to complete the operation.

All very simple when said quickly, but it was a natural sequence and we would start on the nearside by the square.

After lunch Jon and I cut and prepared the two wall plates, and the two support timbers which would form the sides. These outside timbers only had one quarter round on the inside, but they were then nailed to the beams so that we had the frame work firmly in place for the front half. The support timbers were long enough to reach the apex from the wall plate and would tie the whole thing together.

Treating and colouring the new timbers as we went, and standing them aside to dry, we soon had the ten that were needed for the first side prepared. We would work off the bedroom floors, so the scaffolding and ladders were taken upstairs and placed in position.

When building, some of the work had an immediate visual impact; the completion of the roof itself was one of these moments. The transformation is enormous, and seems to appear so quickly; exciting and inspiring.

Well, we started with Jon handing up each part as required, this first section would be the example of these timbers in position. "Plasterboard next please" I asked, then dropped it into place onto the quarter rounds, pushed it flush and then nailed it to the beams. Fantastic!

"A roll of insulation next please" which I unrolled down the centre Wow! I said "another timber please" and so we advanced slowly and surely across the roof. "Dave is going to get a shock when he gets back" said Jon; from the square it looked as if the whole roof was being covered, but actually, of course, it was just one side. Nevertheless the process was working very well indeed.

By the time Dave and family drove back through the square we had but one section left at the front which was a bit harder to reach, but eventually after easing the nailing on the side of the beam which was a bit tight, the plaster board slipped in and the insulation unrolled and now we would be ready to board it over, then felt and batten.

34 - A Roof Sandwich

(Would you Believe It?)

On Dave and Trish's return, they had paused in the car on the far side of the square before driving into the garden, they couldn't believe the change. After lifting out the heavy items from the car, Dave left his family to put away their shopping, and returned to help. "What's next", he said pulling off his shirt and on with his working shorts. I replied that I wanted a small mix of cement, and a bucket of narrow stones about three centimetres in size to infill the front and side walls before this area of roof was boarded in.

The outside boards would sit on these stones which would make it vermin proof, which included little squirrel like creature, to which Dave added "damn right". We would get the boards on, with the stones and cement on the edge, as we worked up the roof. Dave decided that as we only needed a small mix, he would do it by hand and having a quick glance at the consistency, I remarked, "a little more lime Dave and make it quite damp".

It was great progress, the shouting of measurements to Jon; the movement of timber, and the ring of hammers on nails was unremitting. The boards themselves were of random width but averaged approximately twenty centimetres, so the progress up the roof was quite speedy, and when nearly at the top we checked the point where it would meet at the apex, not too snug, a little gap would assist the adhesion of the crest tiles when cemented into place.

Dave said. “Right, now for the other side”, “No” I said “we will felt and batten this side first as a precaution against a thunderstorm”, though none seemed imminent I would not risk the insulation and plasterboard getting wet at this stage.

So the felt and battens were next, always remembering, double depth battens on the front row. This would tip the first line of tiles up a little, to slow and prevent descending water arriving too fast into the gutter. The battens are set at the width of the tile fixing and once measured are stepped in equal distance apart all the way up the roof.

At the end of that day we had the first half secured and waterproofed. A great achievement and I was guessing that this huge progress was being observed from the Mairie, with perhaps disbelief, horror or amazement.

So “tomorrow is another day” as was stated in that wonderful film, “*Gone with the Wind*” and I needed to plan it carefully. There was a “dog leg” in the wall of the cemetery and to allow for this, and to achieve a level gutter one has to raise the angle in the roof at this point. Technically OK but not easy to assess: First cut the wall plate at the angle of the “dog leg” and splice together, place it on the wall, then check the whole length for level. The support timbers at this point would need to be cut at the middle beam to achieve what I will call a widows peak. This will mean that the plasterboard for this piece would have to be cut as well, never mind it is all do-able.

So here we go again, but first we will load the completed section with all the tiles for the roof. Come on gang we need a chain again; we all spread out, and the tiles were soon arriving at the top, where we stacked them in a huge line along the crest of the roof. Now we could continue with the back half, knowing that the tiles were already up and waiting for us. Of course with Dave's arrival, there were three of us to continue with the work and the system was well practiced and we were soon up to the "widow's peak".

Two timbers had to be cut again, so offering one up for measuring and marking, I handed it back down to Jon to cut, who, having done so passed it back.

Well, it slipped out of my hand, and then dropped straight back down and landed square on the top of his head.

He yelled - and dropped to a crouch clutching his crown with both hands.

I, of course, could do no better than start laughing - I had not checked as to whether he was really hurt, but I was shaking with laughter.

Eventually when I came down he stood, swung round and kicked me in the shin with a booted steel toecap, and when seeing the expression on my face change from laughter to puzzled pain said "It's not quite so funny now is it?"

I tried to put a good face on it, but he had really put some force in to it and I was so cross (and hurt), that I can still remember it now! Lesson learned I think!

So now the other "widow's peak" (on the roof, not Jon's poor bonce – which now sported an impressive lump) needed some attention.

We had cut and placed the plaster board, and rolled out the insulation over the area, but to board it in was going to be difficult, and then I thought, we have a sheet of sheer- board (like a good quality hard board) left over from the ceiling of the extension, and if we cut a piece to cover the whole of that awkward area it would surely bend into place. I pinned the top end first and then putting my weight and pressure down on it, nailing and securing as I went, with a little extra nailing to hold it into place and I had no doubt that after a few days up in the sun it would assume its new shape.

The tarred felt and battens were next, ready for the tiles tomorrow. The felt was unrolled and tacked, the battens measured, cut and nailed, the slight distortion of the "widow's peak" disguised and covered, along with rest of the roof.

Suddenly Dave said "what's that?" I turned to look, and saw a very big scruffy dog coming up the path of the graveyard carrying what seemed to be a very large bone. Dave shouted at it and it shot away over the back wall. "Bloody Hell", he said, "I don't want to be here when he brings the head". I could only suggest, having observed but one funeral, that when the cadaver was interred into the tomb, and they sort of shuffled the bones of the predecessors to make room for the new arrival, I guessed that there were one or two left over, or too many for the space. UGH.

35 - The 'Turdologist'

The next morning a car arrived in the square, and a young, studious looking fellow got out. He had a camera around his neck and was carrying a clip board, all very strange. He spent some time looking around the square, and photographed the church, and eventually came around to our side and started taking a series of pictures of the old forge. At the nearest end of the building to us, was an old stone chute going up the side of the wall, to the very top of the three storeys.

To many it would be a puzzle but we knew it to be the waste shute of the garde–robe otherwise known as the WC or toilet. This obviously fascinated him and he spent quite some time poking about at the lower end, and peering up it and taking photos. He had acknowledged us and had nodded and smiled, and we wondered if perhaps he was doing some historical research work in the region, perhaps examining very old property and advising on what should be preserved. Dave said that it was quite obvious that he was a "turdologist" and to us he would always remain so.

Un-Hurd would arrive today, and Sam and Martin the day after. There would be much to-ing and fro-ing which would wake up our very sleepy village, but in the meanwhile we would be tiling a roof. The tiles interlocked, but to further secure them against the high winds and storms of this region, the edges would be further secured with a lime and cement mix. Adding lime was very important with clay tiles, as a pure cement setting was far too hard on its own; the softening nature that lime added made the two materials compatible.

A cord line was fixed to mark the edge of the first row to ensure straightness and then the bottom two rows were firmly cemented as we placed them and worked our way up the roof.

We heard an engine, and saw a van creeping slowly into the square, and yes, an electrician had arrived. There was much shouting and greeting, and he disappeared into the garden in search of a cuppa and the "facilities", his terms not mine.

A head soon appeared at the top of the ladder, and he said that his journey had been uneventful, having had a nights stop at the Limoges services. He said he would get himself a little organised but that he was travelling light. He would unload a number of light fittings and wiring which he had brought with him into the building. Then he would have a quick look around before returning to discuss his programme. Fine I said, and so we continued with our work on the roof.

The tiles, although new, were a soft melange of yellows to light red in colour, and were a bit bright but would soon weather, and blend in to match the other buildings in the village. We were very keen to finish this front side of the roof to get the visual effect from across the square.

By now it was nearly lunch time and we were not far from the crest. After demonstrating how that crest would be finished, on reaching the same point on the other side, the last row was placed, and we stood and stretched our backs and shook hands. The remaining tiles needed to be moved over onto the tiled ridge now, as they would be in the way. OK let's get down and have a look.

Un was below sorting through his tools and fittings and we again greeted him warmly, to Dave he was a new acquaintance. He looked a little worn and tired but otherwise was fine, and he walked out with us onto the square to view the finished front of the roof.

We were actually followed by the whole gang, everyone wanted to be a part of this viewing. Much chatter and pointing, and the tile colours in the sun were beautiful. OK. M. Maire you can look now I thought.

After all the practice we had doing the front, the back half went very smoothly, just a small amount of cutting and adjustment to clear the "widow's peak", and once again we were soon at the crest. This final row of tiles was of a different shape and had to be well cemented on, using the same mix as for the ones on the edges of the roof.

The fixing of the gutter was a simple affair but the "dog leg" at the rear of the property created its own headache. The problem of getting up to it was one thing but using the tombs as supports were quite another. It proved very difficult, but in the end we managed to erect some scaffold around and beside them.

We did need to be close to this work. The gutter supports were soon in place and the bend of the "dog leg" was achieved by an angled joint, one short piece of gutter and a stop end completed that section. We then cut the downpipe which ran to the gutter of the extension which proved reasonably easy and the guttering was complete.

Dave and Jon were looking up, and said in unison, "it slopes the wrong way". "No" I said "that is an optical illusion created by the dog leg". Just at that moment M. Turdologist came around the corner, looked up at what we were discussing, shook his head, wagged his finger in its general direction and said "il ne marche pas" (it won't work).

I asked Jon to pass up the watering can that was by the tap at the cemetery gate. He half filled it and passed it up, and, I did enjoy the next bit. I poured water into the gutter at the far end of the "dog leg", Mr

Professor still stood shaking his head, and then very soon the water ran into the gutter.

His face was a picture, a moment of triumph, and I said to Jon and Dave, never forget that the spirit level does not lie. Our gutters were up, and yes, the roof was finished.

36 - A Complete Team

Just on 6:00 PM another vehicle arrived; it was Sam and Martin and they pulled up by the Pegg's, and wandered across to say hello. Neither had met Un before, but soon everyone was getting on fine. A cup of tea was immediately organised; with such a big gathering all the women would assist with the big cook up later to celebrate their arrival, and of course, the completion of the roof.

Mum had taken up where Tacey had left off and become Alex's sous-chef and chief bottle washer. The new, large BBQ would get a good initiation tonight, eleven in number if my recollection is right. Dave, Trish and girls were staying until the weekend as the little-uns wanted to spend some time by the seaside this year. Dave would help with some pointing in the remaining couple of days, he said, and Jon had been invited to a party and I think there were girls to see!

The air was beginning to feel very heavy again, and we all thought that very likely another storm was brewing. The shower in the garden, and bathroom felt the strain of the numbers tonight, but once a rota was organised it all went smoothly. Un was a bit reticent about exposing himself in the garden, but after remarks like "Even your best mates wouldn't tell you..." he did slip away to the bathroom at the end of the queue and came back looking refreshed.

A grand social evening was had by all, and we had woken up The village from its slumbers once more. We had noticed as the light dimmed, little bats flying out from under the front tiles of the under hang. In only one year they had inhabited our cottage, and the children were counting them as they flew out. "Wow!" they said, 35 had flown out to feed – a proper little colony had formed.

Mum said, "Get to it you little chaps, eat as many as you can"; she had been bothered by mosquitoes before settling to sleep the night before, and had us all in stitches when she went mad with a fly swat in the awning. Whack Whack! "You little devils" she was saying, absolutely hilarious!

After the meal that night there were many hands on deck for the washing up, and later Mum picked up the washing up bowl and went to whoosh it over the hedge at the bottom of the garden. Well obviously not a very good whoosher as it turned out, she got rid of some of it, and in her enthusiasm and effort spun around, not only depositing the rest of the water over us, but as an added bonus delivered a very loud fart!

It was the climax of the whole graceful movement, and reminded me very much of that song by Tom Lehrer "*When Rover Got Run Over*" – "They awarded the driver, because of his grace, both ears and the tail....".

Fortunately, Mum saw the funny side as well, and the whole village rang with our laughter.

Trish told us later, that one of the little girls had laughed so hard that she had wet herself.

We did wonder what the mayor and his family would make of this hilarity, and how long ago it had been since such a party had occurred here.

These memories will always bring back a smile to our faces, and as we cleared and then settled that night, we could hear a grumble of thunder starting deep in the Pyrenees. This heaviness in the air would clear after the storm, and in the morning, after the inevitable rain, the dust would be laid and everything washed clean.

As Sam and Martin made their way unsteadily back to the Pegg's, and Un was preparing his mattress in the back of his van, the lighting started to flicker and the sound of the thunder started moving slowly nearer.

Two hours later it finally arrived, spectacular as ever. The God Thor was venting his disapproval and, or discomfort once more. This tempestuous thunderstorm seemed to turn and return as if it were having a huge examination and subjugation of this it's home territory.

As expected the following day dawned clear, fresh and clean; the air reflecting this celebration, as once more the renewal was complete.

Everybody moved in a kind of daze that morning, but as routine governed our actions the beauty of the transformation lifted us all, and the chatter at breakfast was starting to liven up. Un remarked that the drumming of the rain on the van during the night had been quite alarming at times, but he had been so tired that he had rested quite well.

Sam and Martin were lodged on a B&B basis so we wouldn't expect to see them until later. Mum said that she had been a little concerned that the awning would come down, but in spite of some pooling in one corner all was well. I pushed it up to allow the water to run off so that it might dry in the sun. We decided that it might be more sensible if she now slept in the extension for the rest of her stay.

After breakfast and coffee, Dave, Un and I went over the work for today whilst inspecting the site. Dave said "I guess it's muck for me" (Meaning cement) "for pointing", I just nodded.

Un then produced a stick of chalk and after consulting with me the position of the electric points; he marked the walls for sockets, switches and heavy duty outlets. Jon meanwhile was getting ready to spend a day with his new French friends, leaving us to face another working day.

Walking around the inside of the house with Un and Dave, it was a real pleasure to see, that, with the new roof on, everything was dry after such a heavy nights rain. The three of us stood for a moment to appreciate the feeling of our new living space. Not having been a part of the rest of this build, it didn't mean so much to Un, but to Dave and I the amount of extra living area that had now been created was fantastic, and we both marvelled at just how big it now appeared.

"Dave, move the cement mixer nearer to the sand, we need a good soft limey mix, and don't forget the dye!" I said, then turning to Un "We will continue to mark the positions of the plug work and lights etc. Alex is going to need more lights in the kitchen area, but most of the illumination in the downstairs area she has asked to be from wall lights or table lights to make it as simple as possible”.

The power feed line would be boxed in upstairs for the bedside and bathroom lights when complete. I pointed out to him the conduit that took the power under the base floor, and he asked “Was it jointed anywhere under there?” and I replied “I have no idea, because it had already been laid when we bought the property”.

“OK” he said, “I will have to check that out first.” which he did, and then said “There is a problem with this – it is shorting out somewhere under the floor, the circuit has been compromised, which suggests that water has at some time entered the conduits.”

After a quick discussion we decided that we had no other option but to cut that line off, and take the power where it was needed on the surface instead. I said that if he marked the position of the new line it could later be buried and disguised by our pointing.

The work was soon in motion once more, and after the mixing, Dave would cut out the grooves for that electricity line, and I asked Un to sort out a feed so that we might install the water heater as soon as possible, because (by now) we all fancied a proper shower.

“Shall I put in some plumbing at the same time?” asked Un, “I see that the pipe work is available and I could use your blow-lamp to plumb in the bathroom”. I knew that he was also an accomplished plumber as well as an electrician, so of course I agreed.

So many tradesman like Un, had developed a ‘radio need’, “I can’t work without some background babble” he said. It was bizarre to hear a melange of English, North African, Spanish and French music ringing through the cottage, amid the curses of “that’s no good” until he found what he thought was a French equivalent to BBC Radio Two, which was (he assumed) playing home requests for pop songs.

The volume was eventually lowered by Dave threatening to throw his hammer at it, but despite this the work continued steadily. Part of the wiring code in France requires all wires to be sheathed in conduit before cement can be screeded directly over it.

Occasionally, Un would require assistance to draw the wires through this conduit. The main electricity feed from the electricity provider was set on the wall of the courtyard, so it was easy for him to place the main fuse box on the other side of that wall in the kitchen. Then he made his calculations about the number of circuit breakers and values for each of them from there. The temporary line would be left for the time being to avoid any interruption to our work.

Dave and I placed sound polythene sheets at the bottom of the walls upon which we were to be working; Dave's to catch the waste from the grooves that he would be cutting, and mine to catch the cement waste from the pointing.

This would not only protect the floor, but also to catch pointing brush off which could be reused in the next mix of cement (Cornish farmers waste nothing!).

This section now having been completed looked magical! A coffee break was called for and the usual ladies inspection followed. Sam and Martin now joined us, having enjoyed a very good French breakfast with the Pegg's and walking through the new lounge and up the stairs, they both agreed that the work which had been completed had transformed the entire space.

37 - Wiring, Plumbing and Flooring

The water tank had to be lifted in and out, two or three times until Un was sure of the correct fixing position. Not too difficult as it sat on a kind of cradle or stool. It fitted there fine in the bathroom/hall corner and would be very easy to box in later. The emergency waste and drain pipe would connect through the wall to the hand basin waste, which would continue on to take away the shower water. Special provision would be provided for the upstairs drainage and, Un said the electricity feed could follow the same line.

Lunchtime, and all had gone well during the morning, and we were explaining to Un about the influx of people the village would expect at the weekend for their summer fete, and also that as he was more exposed to the noise at the front of the cottage, it might be better if he drew his van into the entrance of the garden.

He had a look but decided that as it was a slope that it might be better off staying where it was. The activities were beginning to start with the organisers of the fete arriving with tractors and lifts, and bunting going up around the square.

Waves of greeting from old acquaintances, and the thumbs up from many of them at the progress on the cottage was amusing; we could tell that now we had celebrity status!

Martin had taken over as first assistant to Un today, so another pair of hands available. Dave had tried to help with the pointing but there is a bit of a trick to it which he could not master, and after many attempts, he started throwing the cement at the wall with his hands, cursing profusely as his effort inevitably fell once more to the floor. He exclaimed in great frustration "I will have to do something else!"

I looked around and eyed the twenty or so bundles of floor boards stacked near the kitchen and said "Right Dave, take a dozen upstairs, and put the rest in the sitting room - we will lay it next week".

“Righty-oh” he said, well pleased with this change.

“Try to keep your stack this side, near to the staircase please, as we will start the flooring at the front of the building both downstairs and up” I indicated.

“What do you hope to finish before you leave this year?” he asked.

“Well apart from the floors, there are 5 wooden sills for the windows to be made and fitted, and upstairs the partitions for the little bathroom with two cottage doors, not to mention some sort of patio in the garden.”

“My goodness!” he said, “You don’t expect much do you?”

“Not really, but now I can see the end of this project approaching, I am eager to get it all finished as soon as possible”.

By the end of that week (and before Dave and family departed) Un and Martin had continued the wiring and had brought it up to date, this included outside lights, kitchen sockets, downstairs bathroom fittings and power points - oh and a light in the hall...

A line feeding the power had been taken through to the cottage for both downstairs and up, making sure the ends were sealed so that they would be available when needed. The plumbing and waste had been finished in the downstairs bathroom and a pipe joined and in place for upstairs as well. Great Progress!

The village music started as usual on the Friday night, and then on Saturday morning we asked Un if they had tuned it to the right program. He smiled at our ribbing and then said that he had eventually got to sleep, but kept being disturbed by running water. We looked at him quizzically. He explained that the side and corner of his van had created a quiet and dark spot for people with a certain need and we all laughed.

The day of the fete meal broke fine, it was to be hot for their celebrations, and there was much to-ing and fro-ing with materials and equipment. There were bakers vans, butchers vans, and tractors with loads of logs;

they needed to light the fire early to be sure of a good depth of glowing embers to heat their very large BBQ.

So, for all our team, a short day of work was organised so everybody could prepare for the nights festivities. Dave and Trish were already packing for their departure tomorrow, and we were wondering how easy it would be for them to cross the square in the morning after the dancing and before the "clearer uppers" had been in. We guessed it would not be a problem.

The internal shower was now in action, albeit with a surround curtain, the tiling would have to be finished at another date, but it would be a great help to cope with the numbers that would require it later this afternoon.

Four o'clock and people were already starting to gather in the square, with many children tearing around in great excitement: Their mothers shouting at them knowing that their smart clothes would be soiled within ten minutes. I told Dave's daughters that if they wanted to do a serious amount of observing they could look out of the window of the cottage upstairs; this was a huge vantage point.

The smells of cooking lamb were now permeating the whole village and by 6:30 we had gathered for our aperitifs in the garden. Kirs for the girls, ice cold beers for the lads, just the job!

I had seen Paul the farmer a little earlier and he said that demand for the tickets for the meal was up on last year, and I jokingly suggested that if they used older sheep the numbers would not be so high. For me, in French, this was very difficult which lead to a great deal of laughter, and which seemed in some way to include an old ram!

It was a splendid evening the meal as wonderful as last years; many toasts were drunk with this one and that, but very sadly, the Mayors presence was never apparent. I touched on this subject with Paul, and he just looked at me a little wryly and gave that French shrug that can mean so many things.

As the coffee came out we were rather bemused to observe many of the older men start to produce unlabelled bottles that had been secreted about their persons. Puzzled by this I enquired of Paul what was going on; this was followed by a finger tapping on the side of his nose as doses were added to our coffees. It was homemade eau de vie; however, there seemed to be a bit more to it than just enhancing the coffee, as it appeared that it was almost a competition to see who had created the strongest!

Fat, full and feeling the effects of the eau de vie, we finally struggled back to our seats in the garden, and we offered a nightcap, or another coffee before turning in. Dave and Trish declined "I am driving out to the coast tomorrow, best not to", he said. "I think it will take about four hours to get to there, and then we will slowly work our way up to the port from there." Alex and I knew the area well, and said that the Brittany coast in good weather was beautiful, the fish amazing, and the beaches great; but they were planning to follow the coast up from Bordeaux.

As expected the next morning, the square looked as though a bomb had hit it, and as Dave and family drove over and around the debris with all of us waving, Un appeared from his van looking a bit groggy. He said that it had been well past four in the morning when the music had finally died away, adding (hopefully), that perhaps it would be a little quieter earlier tonight.

Today of course would be the boules competition, and Martin (bless him) thought it would be fun if we entered as a team. Well this turned out to be a bad decision, as the worst that could have happened actually did. Sod's law, we were drawn against a women's team, who quickly proceeded to wipe us out. We could only watch and marvel at their business like intent and accuracy, and we retired bruised and battered.

Afterwards we sat quietly in the garden having a cup of tea and talking about the nature of the area: We had noted, for instance, that less than half of our colony of bats had returned after the last storm, and discussed how their sonar might have been affected by the noise and electricity generated by it. Most of them, Martin said, would have been totally disorientated, lost and then drowned in the following downpour.

We then turned to talk about the little squirrel type beasty that lived in the wall of the cottage. Sitting there quietly the night before, we had heard little feet pattering over the newly tiled roof, down along the full length of the garden wall, and disappearing into the cemetery. I couldn't understand where he might have come from, so I had a quiet walk around the back of the cottage, through the cemetery, and there high above the mayor's family tomb was a little hole in the wall.

He must have been climbing up over to the new roof, then, following along the gutter to the garden wall. Not a welcome tenant, they are notorious for getting into roofs and causing a lot of inconvenience and are expensive to dislodge.

Martin thought for a while and then said "I have a cunning plan! I will make an Extremely Dangerous Killing Machine..."

His idea included a scrap of floorboard, a biscuit tin, and a light fitting with a bulb in it. He cut the tin into an interlocking grid, in such a way that should something step on it, it would necessarily complete an electrical circuit and receive an electric shock. The bulb, he explained, was to make sure that the electricity would continue to flow should the trap be tripped without blowing a fuse.

Electrician Un realising that we were planning something, left his work and said "What on earth are you chaps doing?"

Martin showed him and explained what it was all about. Well, here we have an electrical safety officer of the BBC, and very qualified electrician discussing the "*Extremely Dangerous Killing Machine*".

"Fine, fine said Un, let's just hope it doesn't rain as we all know that water and electricity don't mix".

The most obvious position for it to be placed would be on the wall where beasty comes down, and as a concession to safety, Martin said he would make sure that it was connected to an RCD (Residual Current Device).

Finally it was fabricated, finished and fitted; it was time to test it. UN produced his testing kit, and plugged it in. He then said “Blimey Martin, you’ve done a good job there, its bloody lethal!”

The “EDKM” was carefully put aside to be set later that evening.

With the tiredness of “fete hangover” our progress had slowed a little, but I thought that I would like to play with some wood!

So, on to the window sills; I used floor boards slotted together, glued and cut into shape with the outside edge nicely rounded and checked for an exact fit. I then prepared the stone sill with an inch of lime and cement, nailed nine millimetre short nails which I had left protruding from the bottom of the boards, and having positioned these boards, pressed them firmly down onto the cement.

Bingo! The window was transformed by this addition and was now finished in a very classic cottage style.

After the meal that night, it was back to the positioning of the killing machine and as the sky slowly darkened we all strained to hear little beastie on the tiles...

Finally, yes, there it was, pitter, patter, pitter, patter and we held our breaths; and then “Yeep” followed by, “Flop” over the cemetery wall.

“Gotcha!” exclaimed Martin under his breath.

We grabbed the torch and hurried down the path of the grave yard to find... nothing, not a sign, but what is more we never saw or heard him again. Martin thinks that he is still running!

It really surprises us that, after all the crowds of the fete, and after the rapid clean up, removal of debris and the decorations, how quickly this little village slumps back to sleep again. The laughter and music had just faded away once more. It had been a glorious day and as it darkened it turned into one of those velvety nights, the night sky was fantastic, no light pollution here to blind its beauty, and we all gazed at the canopy, it was awe inspiring, and so many stars marking the Milky Way. How insignificant we all are.

Our attentions turned the next morning to the upstairs floor, and as I mentioned earlier Dave had already stacked the floor boards there, and we would start laying them from the side facing the square. Jon and Martin would feed me the materials, one cutting and the other passing those to me as I nailed them, and we were very quickly making progress across the area.

Using disguised nail heads, the colours and the grain of the wood looked beautiful in the local pine that we were using. When the upstairs is finished we will continue with the floor below "Great work chaps, in another day or two this task should be finished" our schedule was progressing well, and in fact we had moved downstairs towards the end of the first day.

Un who had been working in the kitchen had a quick look around for any of his tools, as he was also leaving today, and was mightily impressed with the finish of the floor. After many thanks, and farewells, left us to return back up the road to the port. His contribution had been invaluable and apart from giving us the comfort of a near complete bathroom had proved the 'dodgy electrics' not only safe but had replaced them totally.

38 - The Sunday Trip

(To the River Aude & Limoux Wine Fair)

Our little village is located right in the centre of the department of the Aude, which of course takes its name from the river, which as yet we hadn't actually seen.

It was time to rectify that omission and as our helpmates had been reduced to two (just Martin and Sam) now would be a splendid opportunity. Jon would be once more with his French friends on this Sunday, so we decided that the five of us would go off exploring. A day break away from the work would be so good for all of us, but particularly Alex and Mum, as watching a construction taking place can be less than exciting...

The river rises to the east between our little village and the Pyrenees, so on this Sunday we headed off from the village slightly 'left and up'. As the crow flies it would be about 50 Km, so the plan was to drive towards the river and then follow its path, as it meandered, towards the coast. The river picks up the summer melt from the peaks, which then cascades down the gorges and ravines at speed, and then flows more gently on to Carcassonne and out to the Mediterranean by Narbonne: The river is recorded to be 240 Km in length.

This was beautiful countryside of deep valleys and streams - tortuous driving: One can imagine that many miles of these roads would be impassable in the depths of winter. Really fast water always has a beauty and attraction of its own to me, and there is nothing more fascinating than watching a waterfall, tumbling into a deep pool some metres below.

The water was beautifully clear and icy cold, but we saw nobody bold enough to be tempted to swim in it, but we did see the occasional fisherman, (fishing being an activity close to my heart), but there was little evidence of a catch.

Occasionally we would come across a small village and even a solitary house or two in this wilderness and marvelled; Why? Who, and how had they sustained themselves miles from any other civilisation, particularly in the winter time.

The rivers and the timber would appear to be all the area provided, but was it possible to sustain a living and offer comfort? What problems would occur when children arrived? The thought of sickness, and old age up here would be very difficult.

We were amazed, however, at the general condition of the roads, miles and miles of them, and generally in a fair state of repair. The costs of maintaining this vast network, with the regular rock falls and general winter damage, must be huge.

As we progressed, and crossed and re-crossed the river, we noticed just how many little streamlets were joining it, as tributaries carrying water from the mountain and hill tops, increased the water flow, and of course this just emphasised how the river gets to be so big before it reaches Carcassonne! For several miles we lost sight of the river as the road continued towards the north east, but always knowing that we would intercept it again when it reached the lower levels.

We eventually arrived at a small village, the road was widening now, and signposts indicated that we were approximately 20 Km from Limoux. A coffee stop at a cafe and a chance to review our trip so far; it soon became evident that few visitors, and even less English called here, but we were able to make ourselves understood. The replies from the old proprietor were distorted by a severe lack of teeth "I don't suppose that there were many dentists locally" said Sam.

We agreed that a loss of teeth would be a calamity, and that extractions were probably done by a member of the family, or even possibly the local blacksmith!

The coffee soon arrived and was poured out of a blackened old pot, but it was good enough to drink (or even strip paint) and after paying and saying our 'au revoirs' we were back on the road.

After another 2 Km we had our first view of the real river Aude, wide, but fast flowing, this was now a true 'sporting' river. I suspected that it would be deep enough for canoeing, and had huge fishing potential! Vast stretches leading to deeper pools; an anglers dream and I viewed it with a semi-professional eye of envy.

We stopped for a while to enjoy the splendour of it, and then followed the valley slowly down to Limoux. Cars, cars and more cars: What on earth was going on? We were approaching the edge of the town; vehicles were parked quite randomly on the verges but eventually we spotted a gap, so quickly pulled in. It seemed that taking the car any further would be pointless, and the only way to find out what was happening would be to walk in.

They were having their wine fair, with all the Limoux 'producteurs' giving everyone a taste of their wares amid much music and hilarity. The ambiance was fantastic - the sparkling wine was particularly good. Alex warned "Go steady driver!" to which I reluctantly agreed. We spent a very jolly hour with these wine sellers, who were determined to make a success of their 'foire'.

We looked over the bridge to the river and spotted some decent sized trout, and then continued to explore some of the back streets. Like many of the other towns we had visited, it was steeped in the history of the area, and oh yes, you guessed it: It was another town where Simon de Montfort had left his mark as the square was named after him; it had been yet another place where he had stamped out the Cathars strengths and beliefs in the period of their persecution.

Returning to our car, we were soon leaving these festivities behind, having bought several bottles of the Blanquette de Limoux, the local sparkling white wine. We needed to find our way back to the main road to Castelnaudary and then on to our little cottage.

39 - The Small Room

(And the Final Work of this Year)

Monday morning, and back to the schedule of work. The next effort being the stud partition walls of the little bathroom upstairs. We lifted the timbers, tools and the workbench up there and into position, we then marked the floor with chalk showing doorways and dimensions; we were ready to begin. Jon asked "How do we start?" to which I replied "With very careful measuring we will make the side wall frame in one piece, and when we had put it into place and secured it firmly, have two parallel walls to work from."

This went according to plan, and fitted well. Checking the vertical, we drilled and nailed it top and bottom. Now we could frame in the rest with two identical doors, one on either side. At this juncture the wiring was added; a wall light, with switches by each door, and a vanity light with a shaver point over the sink. The doors would be fabricated from excess tongue and groove floorboards and would have door latches and hinges of the traditional cottage style.

Now all we had to do was to add the plasterboard and insolate the stud partitions to complete them. It sounds simple, but working in small and tight areas is not that easy, often finding ourselves falling over each other. However having installed the toilet, bidet and hand basin, it was really surprising how quickly this shared amenity appeared.

It would be a great asset, I thought, and would alleviate the normal scramble for the bathroom downstairs. Before completing the plumbing and electrics, I realised that we needed to fix the skirting boards, and skim the walls with plaster before Jon could paint the whole area.

Tacey and her boyfriend Mark would arrive Friday afternoon and would need collecting from Castelnaudary railway station, Sam and Martin were departing on the Sunday, so two in and two out...

It would be good to see Tacey, as we had been away some time - of course we had not yet met Mark. They had planned their holiday so that they would be camping with us for a few days (their tent would be erected on the scar left by Dave's caravan), after which they intended to finish with a trip canoeing in the Ardennes.

We intended to leave a little earlier this year, taking a short break further up in France to further explore a new area. Decisions would now have to be made on the work still to be finished, as we had no wish to chase impossible targets for our remaining time there.

We sat that evening and discussed the progress we had made on this cottage that summer, remembering just what condition it had been in on our first visit. It was now a beautiful little holiday home, and the work had been deeply satisfying, and the weather sublime.

The area, with the backdrop of the Pyrenees was superb for both walkers and nature lovers.

We had no doubt that the region's Cathar history, with its hilltop villages and mountain retreats would be a huge draw for visitors in the future. So in the years to come, as a holiday let, it would have great potential.

This being before the days of cheap air travel, as the main drawback for this location was its distance from the ferry ports – during our summers there we had seen very few foreign number plates. Toulouse airport was a great asset, but at this time flights from Britain were mostly limited to the London airports and quite expensive. In spite of this we had grasped the 'French nettle', and very firmly too; producing the proverbial purse out of a sows ear.

We were now within sight of our departure for the year once more. Un the electrician had gone, Sam and Martin were about to leave, the knowledge that Mark and Tacey only staying for a few days, put it all into perspective:

The garden was showing evidence of all the activity that had taken place; Alex and I were discussing what all this change had done for our lives as we reflected over everything – including our own imminent journey home.

Yes, we were pausing on our return through France, not just to have a break for ourselves. Oh no, but also to look at properties nearer to the port - exploratory only we had said, but we both *knew* just how improved my back and my humour had been in the heat. So who knows?

Sam and Martin left after breakfast, and my word, the quiet that descended on our little corner was very marked indeed.

Working quietly and efficiently Jon and I fabricated the cottage style doors for the bathroom, fitted them, and then applied the plasterboard to the stud partition walls. Now that it was all in place we could see that the division would be fine for the two double bedrooms. Jon had drilled and pulled the wiring through for the bathroom, and with the doors hung with those proper cottage style latches, the whole area looked great.

As we had been progressing, I was compiling a list of requirements for the following years work; the plans for the kitchen were proving problematic.

We had decided to purchase all additional materials for the kitchen in the UK; we had a log burner already waiting to be installed, but needed a traditional hearth for it to sit upon, and chimney breast to finish the effect.

The side door into the courtyard would greatly benefit from having a porch; two old oak pillars supporting this would add function and character to that area, and gravelling the courtyard would make the whole area tidy.

40 - Mark and Tacey Head In

(By Train)

Jon would soon be starting a new job in IT for the British government back in England and needed delivering to Toulouse airport; it would make sense that mum travelled with him and both could then be collected by a friend on arrival in England.

Mark and Tacey arrived at Castelnaudary station, and this was a first for a friend or family to arrive in this manner. They had thoroughly enjoyed their swift passage through France this way; they had been able to see a lot more of the countryside; and viewing the changing scenery from this higher perspective emphasised the regional and architectural differences that are evident from the north to the south.

Later, Tacey was showing Mark around the cottage, which had changed so much even from her last visit, and explaining to him how primitive it was at the beginning of the operation. He was mightily impressed, and was looking forward to making a small effort of his own, before continuing their holiday. He had expressed a willingness to help in any way, and I thought, that to assist with laying the patio leading from the large glass doors would be a major contribution.

We had a bundle of battens left over from the roof, quite a pile of sand, some dye and several bags of white cement. Mark was keen to know how we would go about it. I explained that we would fabricate a lattice frame of squares with the battens, set them level at the correct height, then infill with a wet mix of dyed cement. Only when totally dry would we carefully remove the battens before pointing in the joints. "Ahh!" he said, "It will look like laid slabs."

"That's the general idea" I replied, "but practice makes perfect".

The cutting and nailing for the frame went well enough, and it was bedded onto a small layer of cement to ensure it was level. Mark enquired how long it would be before we could remove the battens "Sadly not until after you have left, and maybe not until next year" I admitted.

The time for the great tidying up had arrived, and the task of securing the property would soon be upon us once more, and in no time we would be moving off. Tomorrow we would be delivering Jon and Mum to Toulouse so they could catch their flight, and as Mark wanted to visit the medieval city of Carcassonne, we decided to do that the day after.

41 - A Day in Carcassonne

The route to Carcassonne down the valley to Narbonne was becoming quite familiar to us, but as a retired farmer it always gave me a thrill to see the changes that the different seasons have on the crops.

To me all these changes seemed to happen so much faster than they do in England, as one would notice colour variance week to week; suddenly a barley crop would be ready to harvest, or indeed had already been removed. Then their huge combine harvesters do the summer circuit, starting with oil seed rape, then the winter sown cereals (barley and wheat), before ending their season with maize, sunflowers and millet.

If there was any time between these harvests, many of the farmers would break open the newly harvested ground and commence preparation for the next year's crop. All this is filtering through my mind as we passed down through the valley. To other people it would just be the constant change of colours that come with this sequence of crops and culminating in the autumn with the added mix of the exotic colours of the foliage of the vines and the associated excitement of the advancing '*vendage*'.

Passing the town of Bram reminded us of the '*contretemps*' we had with our mayor, but time was softening that memory, as we all felt that our presence had now become accepted as he and his family had slowly realised that we didn't have two heads; the calming and diffusing strategies we had employed had obviously worked, as we were now part of the village summer scene – almost certainly a source of interest and conversation.

This valley would now always remind us of the happy moments of our time here; incredible thunderstorms and the very slow progress of other visitors discovering this beautiful but remote corner of France.

We soon spotted Carcassonne lying away to the west, and as it had become a world heritage site, we wondered how many other tourists there would be coming to visit this great monument to French history in the south.

It is a fortified city; its strategic location recognised as far back as Roman times. Since then significant extra fortifications were added by successive generations, and was key to many power struggles over the ensuing centuries.

Sadly, when no longer a frontier city, it fell into disrepair, however, significant restoration was undertaken; a great deal of work had been achieved in the last century. Not all of the restoration looks authentic, but I imagine the cost of the renovation would always have been an issue.

We spent two or three hours wandering the narrow streets within the walls of the '*cité*' and were amazed at its size and condition. Tacey and Marks enthusiasm and curiosity having been satisfied by having seen all they wished, we met up later to explore the contents of an ice cream shop, after which we returned to our car.

We now planned to head up into the Pyrenees to find a picnic spot with glorious views before returning along the foothills.

The city had been busy with visitors, but very quickly we escaped the bustle of traffic; winding through the narrow roads up in to the scrub, vineyards and dilapidated farms with small fields. Apart from the vines, some had poor cereal crops, and here I had my first and last sighting (in France) of a crop of black oats, which had been so favoured as horse feed on the farms in the UK during the last war. We all have a store of memories that can be triggered by such events; it reminded me of my maternal grandfather, and also the farm of my childhood growing up in the Westcountry.

We soon found a suitable area to drive into for our picnic with a superb view down over the old city and the road to Narbonne. There was little cover here, but spotting a small bush, Alex said "I badly need a wee, keep guard and warn me of any approaching vehicles"

"No problem" I replied.

Almost immediately I became aware of a strange noise; it certainly wasn't an engine. I listened to it attentively, but couldn't work it out; it was a sort of '*swish swish'* noise.

Suddenly a *peloton* of bicycles came round the corner! I shouted a warning and had a vision of Alex rushing toward the car with her knickers around her ankles! Mark and Tacey were clutching themselves with mirth. I still can't watch the *Tour de France* on the television, without it bringing a smile to my face as that memory floods back to me.

As we climbed further up the slopes, more and more vineyards came into to view; some very run down, but others well managed. We were now driving through the Corbières wine region.

At this time it had not yet achieved the prestige of AOC, but it was obvious that some of the *domaines* were moving in that direction. Quite a dark, full bodied red wine which leaves touches of flintiness at its finish. I really enjoyed it, and it has remained a favourite ever since.

We visited one of the largest *domaines* which turned out to be a convent sanctuary, and discussed the solitary life and hardships they must have experienced from their daily regime, combined with the work of the vineyard itself.

A sample of their wine was duly purchased, and we proceeded on our way through several sad little villages with many of their buildings in ruin, and felt that within a very few years that some of them might cease to exist at all.

Making our way slowly back towards The village we passed some road signs for a Dominican Convent at Fanjeaux that had a lot of history, and we felt that a visit would complete our day out.

The approach was through an avenue of plane trees on a gradient up to this fortified village. There was a viewing point at the top in the square and from this height we could see for miles and miles across the plateau, which no doubt, included our village and all points east.

The convent itself was at the other end of the village, and visitors were asked to ring the bell by the big doors. Having pulled the handle we heard a 'dong' deep within the building, and before long a nun arrived and greeted us in French. After our reply, she asked "Vous êtes Anglais?"

"Oui" we responded.

She was so delighted to welcome us, explaining that they didn't get many English visitors and that an English sister 'Julia' would be delighted to meet us and show us around. She ushered us in and asked us to wait, which of course we did.

After a short while she returned in the company of a tiny, birdlike nun who grasped our hands in welcome saying in a beautiful cut glass voice "I am so very pleased to meet you, my name is Julia Hansard, and I am the last of the Hansards".

We knew immediately who that family was; they were (and the company is still named after them) the recorders of events in the Houses of Parliament. What an extraordinary meeting – she was wonderful, leading us around the building and explaining all about the community that lived there, and their connection with the history of the region.

This ended our day out on a very memorable note, giving us a lot to chat about on our return back for our evening.

42 - Mark and Tacey Head Out

(And We Head up to the Quercy)

Mark and I had finished the patio, it looked really professional and he had gained much satisfaction having been able to make a contribution to the work.

Their train would be leaving in the morning, and their packing was complete so they could strike camp early. We had really enjoyed seeing Tacey and meeting Mark. She had been overwhelmed by the progress that had been made on the cottage, admitting that we had more imagination over such things than she did! Alex and I together drove them in to Castelnaudary, neither of us had waved farewell to a train in many years.

The general clearing up of the site was nearly finished, as we had been gradually tidying for several days, and so next year we would just need to finish the fireplace, kitchen, and porch and the cottage renovation would be completed. There was now very little left to linger for – our busy workplace looked and sounded deserted, which of course it was!

As we left our village we headed north to the old city of Cahors which was situated on a big curve of the river Lot, and as I have mentioned, we intended to spend a few days there before heading back to Blighty.

We guessed that this first leg of the journey would take approximately three hours; using a guide book Alex had already located a caravan site close to the river.

At that time the road to Cahors was still situated on a Route National (rather than an Autoroute), so the journey wasn't very fast as we were also competing with lorries all the way.

We were passing through peach, nectarine and melon country; and there were many road side producers, selling trays of fresh fruits and we pulled in to buy a selection for our enjoyment at our next stop.

Driving off the chalk high ground and drifting down towards Cahors with the main line railway skirting the hill to our right, we arrived in the Lot valley. It was an ancient city, and the roads through it proved to be very difficult, especially towing a caravan; it was stop, start, traffic lights, roundabouts, and then a narrow bridge!

Halting by one traffic light opposite a café, we saw a group of boisterous youngsters '*en fête*' as it were; suddenly without warning there was a loud BANG! One of them had thrown a firework under the car, and they were laughing at our reaction. The proprietor arrived outside and gave them a good old verbal bashing, at the same time raising a hand of apology to us as if to say youthful "Exuberance and Beer".

We proceeded slowly up through the main street, eventually bearing off to the left heading in the direction of Villeneuve-sur-Lot, continuing until we came to a small village called Prayssac.

Alex had already a selected the campsite for our short stay (from the Caravan Club Guide) near the river, and once it was located, we were installed with our BBQ ready for me to cook upon in no time at all: Because, as everyone knows, men do the barbequing.

The sky looked as though a storm might be brewing, and on this occasion it arrived before the cooking was completed. One can feel a bit of an ass standing cooking at a BBQ with a brolly in one hand, and BBQ tongs in the other, however we had to agree that the guinea fowl was superb!

Whilst we were sitting under the awning enjoying our meal, we were also treated to the entertainment of watching other campers on the site scurrying around attempting to keep the torrents of water out of their tents...

The next morning we drove down beside the river, and arrived at the small town of Puy-l'Évêque. It sits upon a bluff overlooking the Lot, and has wonderful views across acres and acres of vines dotted with the occasional field of maize or sunflowers.

The Cahors pressing is known as 'the black wine'; historically highly prized by the Romans, Royals and indeed even a Pope or two. The Lot River was large enough to be navigable all the way from here to the coast at Bordeaux. This area was so different from the Aude; Alex remarked "It is so much greener here! I wonder why?"

We strolled down from the top of the town towards the river, spending some time studying the properties for sale, displayed in an estate agent's window. "English Spoken" was also advertised, so we entered, and there before us, sitting at a desk was a dark haired young woman; not unattractive but with a slight turn in one eye that was disconcerting, as it seemed that with the one eye she had you firmly in her gaze, while the other appeared to suggest that it was looking at somebody else over your shoulder!

She spoke very little English, but explained that they had a member of staff who was fluent and who helped with very serious purchasers – eyeing us speculatively. Alex and I exchanged glances, whereupon I explained that we were only on an initial sortie to gain a sense of values, but generally we wished to see properties which had the potential for conversion into holiday accommodation. Irene (it turned out that was her name) said that this was now THE area that visitors were flocking to as the Dordogne had become hugely popular.

The Lot, she suggested was a natural progression towards the south. She also suggested that if we returned the following day she would have sorted out a few properties to view, to help with our assessment of the values of the area. We did see the sense in this and made an appointment to return on the morrow at 10:00 AM.

We spent the rest of that day exploring the area and were very impressed with the architecture, the golden stonework and countryside.

The next morning bright and early we arrived at the office, and were again greeted by Irene who was all of a bustle, explaining that we would complete a circuit to view five or six properties. We would leave our car and she would drive us, which she did to a degree; poor Alex, never the best of travellers, this turned out to be an experience that she has inevitably never forgotten.

Narrow country lanes, beating along with two wheels in the gutter was the way Alex described it, I just held on for grim death, praying that no lorry or bus would be coming from the other direction.

Through the course of that morning we saw four or five properties of different sizes and potentials, the prices varying considerably, but all were certainly more expensive than anything we had seen in the Aude.

Nothing she showed us fitted what we had in mind; they all tended to be big, ugly and completely unsuitable for the holiday trade.

At lunchtime we pulled into the little square of a small town called Cazals, where we searched for a snack lunch, and for me, a cold beer. Irene said that after eating and refreshing ourselves, she had one more property she wished us to see which she felt would be more suited to what we were searching for.

It was (she explained) an old *'fermette'* meaning a small farm; dilapidated, but with barns and some land. I felt much more encouraged by the sound of this, but Alex had experienced just about enough of Irene's driving; pale and drawn she just nodded miserably. Of course she was right to be anxious as we shot up another series of lanes, and clinging on for dear life, we careered into a disused farmyard.

What we were looking at was completely run down, but the main building resembled a Devon longhouse with two barns adjoined, forming a row. Opposite these, there were two nearly roofless buildings which had been stock houses in the past, and all was surrounded by tall dead grasses and weed - nothing new there then.

One area could well have been a vegetable garden; another showed evidence of old vines that appeared to be dead. The front of the first barn had a galvanised lean-to, the yard was on two levels and the long house itself had a large flight of concrete steps leading from the lower half to the other.

"Shall we look inside?" said Irene whilst jangling a set of keys in her hand.

"Of course" we said, so she lead us to the upper floor and explained that the old farmer had lived here on his own for several years before his death, that it had been vacant for some time, but that it was still habitable.

Dingy, dusty, three rooms in a row, but habitable it certainly wasn't. At the end of the corridor was a door that was locked, and Irene said it was dangerous and to stand back; when she opened it a black hole was revealed that just dropped to the floor below. The staircase (if there ever had been one) certainly wasn't there.

These 'two dwellings' overlapped each other, neither had ever been properly finished, but the plus side was that altogether it was big and had exactly the potential we were looking for, with enough work for a lifetime.

The two large barns were basically sound with their roof crests level, which showed that the timbers were solid, they were both full of rubbish, but with imagination could be converted into wonderful holiday accommodations.

I guess that life would have been much easier for us if we hadn't both got this ability to be able to see what they could become.

Alex was in a state of near collapse by the time we returned to Irene's office; by now she had a migraine and was also feeling nauseous. Before saying goodbye we told Irene that we would return the next day, having thought about it.

Having regained our car I drove as gently as I could back to the campsite with Alex reiterating “I will never again travel in a car driven by Irene”...

43 - A '*Lot*' of Decisions

That evening we talked about little else; after agreeing that apart from the farm, nothing that we had seen was at all suitable for our purpose; in particular we discussed the price being asked.

Compared to the other properties that we had viewed, we concluded that a price FF 560,000 was reasonable; the question was how quickly it might sell, as interest was picking up in this area.

We reasoned that it would probably sell quite quickly, and that if we wanted to buy it, would it be possible to raise the capital by January the following year.

They were offering several small parcels of land along with this property which were of no interest to us, so the question was would they sell us the buildings and ground we did want (at a reduced price) and sell the rest separately?

To Alex I said, "I'm not sure, but I believe that neighbouring farmers are offered the land first anyway.

So many questions, so much turmoil. What if? What if! If a deposit was paid now, would they wait until the spring for a completion date? Well possibly. We made a list of these queries but little more could be done before the morning meeting with Irene.

The work and effort on our little house in the Aude had been a great success.

It had proven to me that the severe deterioration of my arthritis could be managed with the benefit of really warm weather and some exercise.

Perhaps perspiring heavily had helped to expel the natural acid build up, or never being cold was part of the secret. But don't knock it, something was working in my favour, as I was feeling better than I had for years, and I wanted more of this remedy.

In the morning we arrived at Irene's office to talk about the farm and get answers to our queries. The first question she was able to clear up very quickly. The off ground did not need to come with it, but in this area this second grade farm land had little value, which would mean that no great reduction in price could be expected.

Together we would look at the map, and add up the total of hectares to give an estimate.

There was an area surrounding the bottom of the farm yard, which we would like to include, and a small field between us and our prospective nearest neighbours, that we would also like to buy.

There were several parcels of woodland, totalling altogether, approximately four hectares.

The original asking price was Five hundred and sixty five thousand francs, and the rate of exchange at that time was around 10.5 francs to the pound. Irene thought that the family might accept an offer of Fifty four thousand, excluding the land we did not want. Alex had noticed a dotted line on the plan which crossed the property below the piggeries and continued down through the woods, and I asked Irene what it might be. She replied that usually this was an indication of an old footpath or postman's route, and we enquired whether it could be nullified. She thought this could be arranged with the local maire, but that she would enquire from the vendors.

We then said that if all these points could be agreed, we would make a commitment to purchase and pay a deposit, and complete later in the year. This did not faze her at all, she just asked if we would sign a contract, and pointed out that there was normally a small interest payment in the case of a delay in completion, but signing now would secure us the property.

Alex and I had a quick consultation, I glanced back at Irene and nodded in agreement!

So quick and so simple, and I had just signed off many more years of my working life. Irene then said that she would organise the Notaire (solicitor) for the business end of the deal on Saturday before we continued our return to England.

We left the office in total shock and some excitement. Here we were, having made a stopover, merely to take a look at another department on our way back to port and now, in just two days, we had committed to buy a property, which we hoped we could convert into a holiday complex.

Was this shrewd judgement, excellent value, a brilliant plan, or just gut reaction and sheer insanity?

We didn't know, but that's what we had just done, and now we would have some very serious financial planning ahead of us.

We had taken this huge step in the second phase of our French adventure, and now we must return home and try to explain our latest madness to our family.

Acknowledgements

My love and thanks to my family; for all their efforts, patience and forbearance, not just in this project (and others) but also throughout the process of the retelling.

Also to Dave and his family for added the muscle and company on the journey...

Special thanks also to our friend Len for the delightful pictures of the two little animals.

The cartoon illustrations were drawn and supplied by Emma Parkinson

Printed in Great Britain
by Amazon

41957462R00106